MALAMANDER

THOMAS TAYLOR
ILLUSTRATED BY TOM BOOTH

WALKER BOOKS

Text and map copyright © 2019 by Thomas Taylor
Illustrations copyright © 2019 by Tom Booth

First U.S. paperback edition 2020

Library of Congress Catalog Card Number 2019939000
ISBN 978-1-5362-0722-4 (hardcover)
ISBN 978-1-5362-1515-1 (paperback)

20 21 22 23 24 25 LSC 10 9 8 7 6 5 4 3 2 1

Printed in Crawfordsville, IN, U.S.A.

This book was typeset in Bell MT.
The illustrations were created digitally.

Walker Books US
a division of
Candlewick Press
99 Dover Street
Somerville, Massachusetts 02144

www.walkerbooksus.com

A JUNIOR LIBRARY GUILD SELECTION

FOR CELIA

T. T.

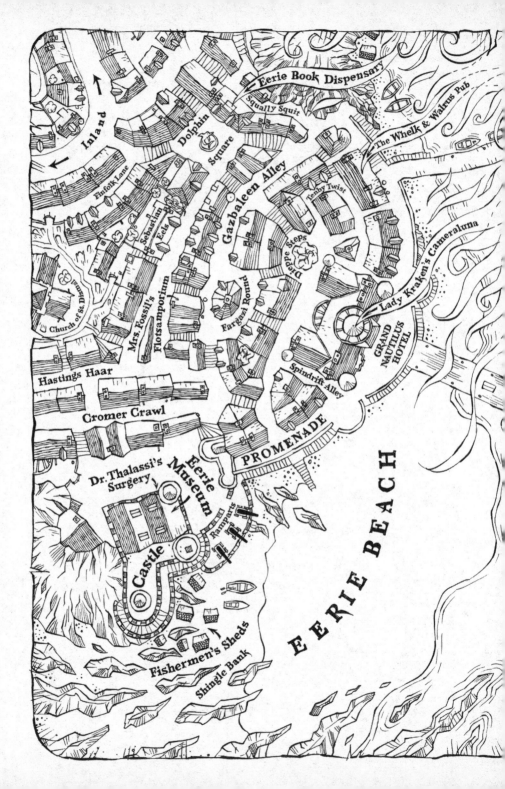

CONTENTS

CHAPTER 1

EERIE-ON-SEA

You've probably been to Eerie-on-Sea, without ever knowing it.

When you came, it would have been summer. There would have been ice cream and deck chairs and a seagull that pinched your chips. You probably poked around in the rock pools with your mum, while your dad found that funny shell. Remember? And I'll bet, when you got in the car to drive home, you looked up at the words CHEERIE-ON-SEA — written in light-bulb letters over the pier — and got ready to forget all about your day at the seaside.

It's that kind of place.

In the summer.

But you should try being here when the first winter storms blow in, when the letters *C* and *H* blow off the pier, as they always do in November. When sea mist drifts up the streets like vast ghostly tentacles, and saltwater spray rattles the windows of the Grand Nautilus Hotel. Few people visit Eerie-on-Sea then. Even the locals keep off the beach when darkness falls and the wind howls around Maw Rocks and the wreck of the battleship *Leviathan*, where even now some swear they have seen the unctuous malamander creep.

But you probably don't believe in the malamander. You maybe think there's no way a fish man can be real. And that's fine. Stick to your ice cream and deck chairs. This story probably isn't for you, anyway. In fact, do yourself a favor and stop reading now. Close this book and lock it in an old tin box. Wrap the box in a heavy chain and throw it off the pier. Forget you ever heard of Eerie-on-Sea. Go back to your normal life — grow up, get married, start a family. And when your children can walk, take them for a day at the seaside, too. In the summer, of course. Stroll on the beach and find a funny shell of your own. Reach down and pick it up. Only, it's stuck to something . . .

Stuck to an old tin box.

The lock has been torn off and the chain is gone. Can the sea do that? You open the box and find —

It's empty.

Nothing but barnacles and seaweed and something else. Something like . . . *slime*?

You hear a sound behind you — a sound like footsteps, coming closer. Like slimy, flippery footsteps *coming closer.*

You turn around.

What do you see?

Really?

Well, maybe this story *is* for you, after all.

THE GRAND NAUTILUS HOTEL

My name's Herbert Lemon, by the way. But most people call me Herbie. I'm the Lost-and-Founder at the Grand Nautilus Hotel, as you can see from my cap. Someone once told me that most hotels don't have a Lost-and-Founder, but that can't be right. What do they do with all the lost stuff, then? And how do the people who've lost it get it back?

I'm a bit young for such an important job, I suppose, but Lady Kraken herself — the owner of the hotel — gave it to me. Even Mr. Mollusc, the hotel manager, can't argue with that. He'd like to, of course — he hates anything in the hotel that doesn't make money. If he'd had his way, the Lost-and-Foundery would have been shut down as soon as he became manager, and my little cubbyhole in the reception lobby would have been boarded up for good. And if that had happened, I'd never have met the girl.

The girl I found scrambling though my window.

The girl who said, "Hide me!"

⚙

"Hide me!"

I look her up and down. Well, mostly up, because she's gotten herself stuck on the window latch, and the cellar windows are near the ceiling. If she's a burglar, she's not a very good one.

"Please!"

I get her unstuck, although that means nearly being squashed as she tumbles inside. It's snowing, so a whole lot of winter comes in through the window, too.

We get to our feet and now I'm face-to-face with her: a girl in a ratty pullover with a woolly bobble hat over a mass of curly hair. She looks as though she's about to speak, but she stops at the sound of raised voices up above. Raised voices that are getting closer. The girl opens her eyes wide with panic.

"In here!" I whisper, and pull her over to a large travel trunk that's been in the Lost-and-Foundery, unclaimed, for decades. Before she can say anything, I shove her inside and close the lid.

The voices are right up at my cubbyhole now — the whining, wheedling sound of Mr. Mollusc trying to deal with someone difficult. I grab a few lost bags, umbrellas, and other odds and ends, dump them on top of the trunk, and hope they look as if they've been there for years. Then the bell on my counter, the one people ring when they want my attention, starts *TING, TING, TING*-ing like crazy. I straighten my cap, run up the cellar steps to my cubbyhole, and turn on my "How may I help you?" face, as if nothing strange has just happened at all.

Mr. Mollusc is the first person I see, trying to smooth his hair over his bald patch.

"I'm sure it's a misunderstanding," he splutters to someone. "If you would just allow me to make inquiries . . ."

The someone he is talking to is unlike anyone I've ever seen before. It's a man in a long black sailor's coat that's sodden with water. He looms over the desk like a crooked monolith, his face a dismal crag, his eyes hidden beneath the peak of a ruined captain's cap. With one stiff finger, he is jabbing the button of my bell as if he's stabbing it with a knife. He stops when I arrive and leans in even farther, covering me in shadow.

"Where . . . ?" he says in a voice that sounds like two slabs of wet granite being scraped together. "Girl. Where?"

"Ahem," I say, clearing my throat and putting on the posh voice Mr. Mollusc expects me to use with guests. "To whom may you be referring, sir?"

The man's mouth, which is nothing more than a wide upside-down V in his dripping bone-yellow beard, opens with a hiss. I notice there is seaweed in that beard, and more is tangled around his tarnished brass buttons. He smells as though something bad is about to happen.

"WHERE?"

I gulp. Well, I can't help it, can I? I'm just a lost-property attendant. I'm not trained for this.

"My dear sir," purrs the voice of Mr. Mollusc, "I'm sure we can sort this out. What exactly have you lost?"

The man pulls himself back out of my cubbyhole and towers over Mr. Mollusc. He draws his right hand, which has been hidden till now, out of his coat. Mr. Mollusc shrinks back when he sees that where the man's hand should be is a large iron boat hook, ending in a long gleaming spike.

"Girl," the man says.

Now, one thing I will say about old Mollusc is that he knows which battles to fight. In this case, since there's no way he can beat this great hulking intruder, he decides to join him instead. He turns on me.

"Herbert Lemon! Do you have a girl down there?"

Now they're *both* looming in at me.

I shake my head. My "How may I help you?" face dissolves, so I try an innocent grin instead.

"No," I manage to say in a squeaky voice. I hate it when my voice does that. "No girls are hiding down here. None at all."

And that's when there's a soft thud from down in the basement behind me. It sounds exactly like someone who is hiding in a travel trunk is trying to make themselves more comfortable.

Oops.

The bearded sailor opens his mouth in a moan of triumph; his dark eyes flash beneath his cap. He yanks open the door to my cubbyhole and shoves me against the wall as he pushes past. He squeezes down the steps to the cellar, filling the tunnel, his back crooked as he stoops beneath the low ceiling.

I hurry after him. This isn't me being brave, by the way. This is just me not knowing what else to do.

The sailor is standing in the middle of the room, commanding the space. I see him look at the patch of melted snow beneath the open cellar window. I see him turn his head to follow the wet footprints that lead straight to the travel trunk. The bags and umbrellas I dumped on it have fallen off. By now there might as well be a big flashing sign over that trunk that reads: YOO-HOO! SHE'S IN HERE!

Mr. Mollusc, rushing down to join the party, sees all this, too, and goes crimson with rage.

"Herbert Lemon! Why, I ought to . . ."

But what he "ought to" I don't find out, because of what the sailor-with-a-spike-for-a-hand does next. He raises his spike and brings it down with a sickening thud, driving it deep into the lid of the chest. He wrenches it out and then swings again, and again. The lid of the trunk splits and sunders, splinters of wood raining down all around. The trunk itself begins to disintegrate. The man tears the rest of it open with the help of his one good hand to reveal . . .

Nothing!

Well, not quite nothing. There's a very surprised-looking spider sitting among the wreckage. And a woolly bobble hat. I watch the spider scurry away and wish I could join it. Now all there is to look at is the hat. It is very definitely the brightly colored hat the girl was wearing. But of the girl herself, there is no sign.

With a slow, deliberate motion, Boat Hook Man skewers the hat on the tip of his spike. He turns and holds it out to me, his face like a thundercloud. Somehow, I find the courage not to squeak as I reach out and gently take the hat from him.

"Just some lost property," I say. "It was, um, handed in this morning. I—I haven't had a chance to label it yet, that's all."

There's a moment of silence. Then Boat Hook Man roars—a great, wordless bellow of fury. He starts ransacking my cellar, sweeping his massive arms from side to side. I fall back to the stairs as bags, coats, hats, lost-thingummy-doodads of every kind—including some that must have lain undisturbed down here since almost forever—fly around. The man is going berserk trying to find the girl. But he finds no one.

She's gone.

CHAPTER 3

VIOLET PARMA

It's afterward, and Boat Hook Man has left. Mr. Mollusc has left too, but not without saying, "Just wait till Lady Kraken hears about this."

I pick up a piece of wreckage from the floor. It's part of the trunk. I'm going to miss that old thing—it's been here for as long as I can remember. Probably no one would have come back for it now anyway, but still, I hate things to be lost permanently.

"Hello?" I say as loudly as I dare, looking around. "Are you there?"

Silence.

I make my way to the window. I should close it—it's freezing in here now—but I decide to leave it open, just a sliver. The snow outside has been replaced by a creeping sea mist, which glides past the window in upright wisps. Like ghosts.

She's well and truly gone, and who can blame her? But I put the woolly hat on the windowsill where it can be seen, just in case.

I start to tidy up, but it's a gloomy business seeing all the poor lost things flung around, and soon I slump down in my armchair in a grump. It's too late to do the job properly now anyway. I look at the little window of my wood burner and see that my first log is flaming merrily. Part of the deal with being Lost-and-Founder at this place is that I get my own stove and a few logs a day. Mr. Mollusc hates this, of course, but he has to lump it because that's how it was when Lady Kraken took over the hotel, and that's how it will always be, I guess. She says it's to make sure that the lost things are dry and ready to be collected, as good as when they were found. And it means that I'm pretty cozy down here through winter, and the fire in the little window is cheery and relaxing and . . .

"Are you going to sleep there all night?" says a voice, and I startle awake.

The girl is sitting on the other side of the stove, the woolly hat in her hands. She raises an eyebrow. I probably look ridiculous as I try to straighten my cap—the elastic has caught around my ear.

"How long have you been there?" I say, noticing that the cellar window is now tight shut.

The girl shrugs, and I get my first proper look at her. She has dark-brown eyes in a light-brown face and a mass of curly hair, which is barely under control. She's probably about the same age as me, so twelve-ish; though, since my own age is pretty ishy, it's hard to be sure. Her bright eyes are quick and amused as she watches me try to suss her out.

She's wearing a too-big coat, and I recognize it as one of my lost things. Her shoes are her own, but they clearly aren't any good for winter and are wet through. I see that the fire has burned low, so I shove another log in.

"Are you a . . . ?" I begin, but she shakes her head, so I try again. "What about a . . . ?" But she just laughs.

"No, none of those," she says. "I'm not a thief, and I'm certainly not a guest at this hotel."

I probably look a bit confused, because she smiles.

"But I know who you are," she says. "You're Herbert Lemon, the famous Lost-and-Founder at the Grand Nautilus Hotel."

"Famous?"

"Well, famous to me. I've come hundreds of miles just to see you, Herbert —"

"Herbie," I say, finally giving up with the cap and taking it off altogether.

"Because I think you are the only person in the world who can help me."

"Really?" I say, scratching my head. "How come?"

"Because I'm lost," she says. "And I'd like to be found."

⚙○❀

There are many strange stories about the Grand Nautilus Hotel, but there's one in particular that I should tell you now. It happened twelve years ago, which is several years before I came here myself, so I'm not exactly a witness. It's the story of a baby found abandoned in the hotel, of parents completely vanished, of strange lights seen from the shore, of police swarming everywhere, searching high and low. Two pairs of shoes belonging to a man and a woman were discovered, left neatly on the harbor wall, along with footprints in the sand, leading from the harbor wall to the sea.

It's a sad story.

Other prints were in the sand, too—funny-shaped markings, as if something with flippers had dragged itself out of the water. But the tide came in before anyone could photograph the marks properly, and that part of the story was left out of the papers.

In fact, all this is hardly a story at all now—more a legend. The Lost-and-Founder before me was briefly involved, but a baby isn't exactly something you can tag and shelve in a hotel cellar, so she got taken away and was never heard of again.

Until now . . .

✿O✿

"OK, I'm going to stop you right there," I say to the girl, because I think I can see where this is going. "Even if you are this legendary lost baby all grown up, I really don't see how I can help. I do lost *things*. Not lost persons. You need a . . . a detective, or something."

"But isn't it your job to find the owner of lost things? How do you do that?"

"Well, sometimes there are clues . . ."

"Exactly! Clues," she says. "You *are* a detective. I'm just another clue."

I sit back in my chair and fold my arms.

"That's not how it works. When I say 'clues' I mean labels and name tags. I mean when someone scratches their phone number on the underside of their suitcase. Do you have a phone number scratched on your underside? No? Well, then . . ."

"But I do have this," says the girl, and she reaches into her ratty pullover and pulls out a folded postcard that she is wearing on a ribbon around her neck. She takes it off and hands it to me.

On one side is a picture of a monkey wearing a top hat. Or is it a chimp? Either way, it's not your regular monkey or

chimp: it has the lower
body of a fish. Printed on the
back is a series of letters and numbers.

I glance at the girl, because this is something I recognize.
But I'm not ready to tell her that yet, in case it sets off the whole
detective thing again.

"It was in my crib," says the girl. "When they found me,
twelve years ago, in one of the rooms of this hotel. Surely you
know something about it, Herbert."

"Seriously, call me Herbie," I say, handing the card back. "Only Mr. Mollusc calls me Herbert."

"Who's Mr. Mollusc?"

"He's the horrible man who will kick you out in the snow when he finds you down here. And me too, probably."

"Don't you mean *if* he finds me?"

"Er, he's already nearly found you once," I say. "And thanks to you, my cellar was trashed by a hideous man with a hook for a hand. So I'm sticking with *when*, thanks."

She looks crestfallen.

"So you won't take my case?"

"Case? *CASE?*" I shake my head in disbelief. "The only cases down here have unwashed underwear in them. You can stay here tonight. It's freezing outside —"

She beams.

"— but I don't take cases, and I don't see how I can help you."

"My name is Violet, by the way," she says, grabbing my hand and waggling it up and down. "Violet Parma. And I just know that if anyone can help me, Herbie, it's you."

It's as if she hasn't been listening to a word I said! I watch as she slips off her ridiculously flimsy shoes and props them by the fire. Outside, the snow has stopped and ice has bloomed across the window. I want to ask her about Boat Hook Man. I want to ask her where she's been all these years. Then I wonder if she's hungry, this Violet Parma, but by the time I open my mouth to ask that, she's already asleep on a pile of coats.

I'm just thinking I should maybe crash out myself —I have a foldaway bed down here—when there's a loud *TING-TING* from up at my desk. It's so unexpected at this time of night that I almost jump out of my skin. I put my cap on and tiptoe up to my cubbyhole, but there's no one there. On the counter is a folded note addressed to the Lost-and-Founder of the Grand Nautilus Hotel. Or, in other words, to me.

I open the note.

Dear Herbert Lemon,

Please come to my room immediately.

Yours sincerely,
Lady Kraken

I gulp. I can't help it. Lady Kraken summons no one to her presence lightly. The hotel runs like a venerable and well-greased machine, with old Mollusc supplying all the grease needed, and then some. Every cog in that machine—from the manager him-self to the most rabbit-eyed chambermaid—knows its place and turns correctly around its particular duty.

Or gets removed.

"Just wait till Lady Kraken hears about this," Mr. Mollusc said earlier.

Well, it looks as if she already has.

My hand is wobbling slightly as I put the CLOSED sign up on my counter. I glance across Reception—empty now this late at night—and catch sight of myself in one of the ancient mirrors. I tug straight the front of my uniform—royal porpoise blue, with a double row of brass buttons—and tuck as many of my scrappy tufts under my cap as I can. I try not to think that this might be the last time I get to wear it.

Then I set off for the hotel's stately brass elevator.

CHAPTER 4

THE CAMERALUNA

I reach the sixth floor, and the doors of the elevator clack open. The carpet here is deep and aqua blue, and the walls are faded coral pink. The ceiling is so far above that I can't see it against the icy gleam of the chandeliers that float there. There are paintings of the Kraken family all along the corridor—admirals and captains from many ages. They stare down at me from decks and staterooms, painted waves crashing against painted rocks behind them.

At the other end of the hallway are the high double doors of the Jules Verne Suite—Lady Kraken's private quarters. I begin the long walk to my doom, passing the narrow bronze spiral staircase that leads to the tower in the exact center of the roof.

I've always wondered what's up there. Now I suppose I'll never know.

Lady Kraken is almost a recluse. All her orders and requests come down via a private elevator, and all her meals go up the same way. In all my years here, I've seen her only a handful of times, and she's famously bad-tempered about having to get involved with the day-to-day running of her hotel.

By now I'm at the door. I reach out a trembly hand and pull the silken rope. I hear a chime like a ship's bell ring out from somewhere. Then, just as I'm wondering if I can sneak off and pretend that no one is in, a light bulb on a brass panel beside the door fizzes on. On the bulb, in tiny curly letters, it reads:

COME IN.

And the door swings slowly open.

The immense room beyond is shrouded in dusty curtains that cover the windows and tumble across the floor likes waves. A conical beam of cold light, swirling with dust motes, descends from the ceiling to a circular table in the middle of the room. Sitting beside the table, in a gleaming bronze-and-wicker wheelchair, is an old lady in a turban. The way her wrinkly head emerges from her sumptuous silky gown reminds me of a turtle. She beckons me in with a motion of her clawlike hand, and the door swings shut behind me.

"Ah, Mr. Lemon," Lady Kraken says as I hesitate by the door.

"Don't just stand there like a question mark, boy. Come closer!"

As I approach, I pull my Lost-and-Founder's cap from my head. The elastic strap pings and nearly takes my eye out.

"Mrs., er, Lady Madame," I say, rubbing my eye and trying a bow.

She lets out a hoot of laughter.

"No need for all that! Come to the table, Mr. Lemon. Tell me what you see here."

I reach the table, which is bathed in the strange shaft of light. It reminds me of a movie projector—only, the light is coming straight down from above. I'm about to ask what it all means when I gasp.

"That's the pier!"

And sure enough, projected on the table in front of me is a moving image of the pier at Eerie-on-Sea, seen from above. But it's not merely a flat picture—the image is three-dimensional, raised up off the tabletop in a structure of sparkling dust motes. It's a perfect model of the pier, with the black sea heaving beneath it.

"Of course it's the pier." Lady Kraken cackles. "And, there, look—Mr. Seegol is just closing up for the night."

And it's true. As I watch I see a tiny model of round Mr. Seegol emerge from his fish and chip shop in the middle of the pier, carrying a bucket. He leans out over the water, which swirls

dark and silver. He stands there awhile, braced against the wind as if listening for something. Then he places the bucket down in the shadows before going back inside. In a moment, the cheery light from Seegol's Diner snaps out.

"Poor man," says Lady Kraken. "Still waiting, I see."

"But what is this?" I say, marveling at the magical diorama. "How can we see this here, on the table?"

Lady Kraken raises one bony finger and points upward.

"It's my cameraluna," she explains. "In the tower. It lets me keep up with the doings of our strange little town."

I blink and don't know what to say. What's a cameraluna?

"Let us pay close attention for a moment," says Lady Kraken, turning a brass wheel on a black control box attached to the arm of her chair. The model of Seegol's Diner grows larger as we zoom in, almost filling the tabletop. But with that it grows fainter, too, and it's hard to see anything clearly now. Lady Kraken leans in closer.

"Now, what, Mr. Lemon, do you suppose *that* is?" And she points her crooked finger at a patch of darkness at one side of the pier.

I lean in closer too, wondering what I'll see, and what's expected of me. The image starts to fade in and out, but then I see it: something darker than the shadows, crouching on the pier. Something big. It begins walking—no, *creeping*—toward the diner. It seems human, until . . .

"Is that a tail?" I gasp.

Two lamp-like orbs blink in the darkness.

"Are those *eyes*?"

"Then you *do* see it?" Lady Kraken grabs my arm. "Mr. Lemon, tell me we're not dreaming!"

The shape rears up, and I see rows of what could be quivering spines and something that might be a grasping claw. But before I can be sure, the image on the table flickers, fades one last time, and then winks out. The shaft of light from the ceiling is extinguished and the dust motes collapse.

"Curse the clouds!" shrieks the old lady, frantically twisting the brass wheel in both directions. But nothing happens. The table is just an ordinary table again, with a thick layer of dust on its surface.

It's very dark in the room now, but there is a paraffin lamp nearby, turned low. I give a polite little cough and turn it up, filling the room with warm light. Lady Kraken is still staring at the table.

"*Did* you see it, Mr. Lemon?" she says again. "Did *we*?"

I scratch my head.

"I saw something," I say, "but I still don't know how I could see anything at all. What's a cam—a cameraluna?"

Lady Kraken lets go of the control wheel and narrows her eyes, as if seeing me properly for the first time.

"There are lenses in the tower on the roof. Special lenses. They collect the light of the moon and project it down here. From the tower I can see the whole town. Well, almost the whole town . . ."

The old lady grasps the paraffin lamp and holds it up. I sense the shadows stretch up behind me as she wheels closer.

"Remind me, Mr. Lemon," says Lady Kraken. "How long have you been here?"

"Um. About five minutes . . ."

"No!" Lady Kraken rolls one wizened eye (but only one). "Don't be a dunderbrain, boy! I mean, how long have you been with us at the hotel?"

"Well . . ." I get my fingers out and tot up the seasons. "Five years. Almost to the day."

"Five years!" Lady K blinks, lowering the lantern. "Is it really five years already? I recall it as if it were yesterday. You were found on the beach, were you not? Washed up in a crate of grapefruits."

"Um, lemons, Your Ladyness," I correct her. "It was a crate of lemons."

"Ah, yes, of course. And you refused to tell anyone your name."

"I couldn't remember my name!" I blurt out. "I still can't."

"Yes, indeed." Lady Kraken nods. "So we gave you one."

I say nothing. Even I have to admit that the name Herbert Lemon suits me somehow.

"And since no one knew what to do with you," Lady Kraken continues, "and since our last Lost-and-Founder had gone missing, we gave you a job, too. I've always felt the post of Lost-and-Founder at the Grand Nautilus Hotel is best fulfilled by a child. And you were our youngest ever."

Here comes the chopping block, I can't help thinking.

"But I wonder, Mr. Lemon," says Lady K, her eyes narrowing till they are almost shut, "are you really happy here?"

I open my mouth to reply "Yes!" but nothing comes out.

Am I happy here?

I mean, *happy*?

My mind dances with images from the last few years—the kind faces of the hotel staff who've watched over me, the regular guests who treat me with affection, the way old Mollusc's mustache twitches in outrage when he sees all this but can do nothing about it. What's not to be happy about? And, yet, there's that crate of lemons. And the mysterious blank in my memory that leads up to my strange arrival in Eerie-on-Sea.

"I can honestly say, Lady Kraken," I say eventually, "that the day you made me Lost-and-Founder was the best day of my life . . ."

. . . that I can remember, I add, but only in my head.

Lady Kraken breaks into a slow smile—one that spreads up both sides of her face and makes her look more like a turtle than ever.

"Ah, good. Then you won't mind if I add a few little extra tasks to your duties, will you, Mr. Lemon?"

And, of course, I have no choice but to nod in agreement.

"Because, you see," Lady K continues, leaning in closer still and lowering her voice, "there is one place in this town that I can't see with my cameraluna, and that's *inside* my own hotel. But you, Mr. Lemon—you could be my eyes and ears, could you not? My eyes and ears, both inside the hotel and beyond. You could be my spy?"

I nod again and manage to suppress a squeak.

"And you would tell me—wouldn't you, Mr. Lemon?—if something strange were to happen in the Grand Nautilus Hotel. You wouldn't keep secrets from me, would you, boy?"

Lady Kraken gives me a long, wrinkly stare that I swear I can feel at the back of my skull.

"You would tell me about any strange visitors you might have had down in your Lost-and-Foundery. A man, for example, with a boat hook for a hand?"

"As it happens, there was someone like that . . ."

"Then it's true!" Lady K gasps. "He has returned!"

"He . . . he said he'd lost something."

"Something?" Lady Kraken's voice is a hoarse whisper of excitement, and she grabs my arm again. "What sort of something?"

"Well, more of a some*one*, actually," I say. "A girl, he said. So I said I don't do *people*, just *things*, so he said . . ."

"A girl?" Lady Kraken leans back in surprise, letting go of me. "What sort of girl?"

"Well, a lost one, I suppose . . ."

"Herbert Lemon." Lady Kraken raises one crooked finger to silence me. "This is important, now. Did he find the girl?"

I look back at her. A small voice in the corner of my mind tells me to be very careful about what I say next. And that makes my actual reply all the more surprising.

"No," I say. "There was no girl."

CHAPTER 5

LOST LUGGAGE

It's the next morning, and I am woken up by the sound of munching. Violet Parma is sitting in the middle of my lost-property cellar, wrapped in a blanket that she is showering with golden crumbs from an enormous croissant. For a girl who doesn't exist, she's making quite a mess.

"Breakfast?" Violet says, pulling a Danish pastry out from somewhere and tossing it to me.

"Where did you get this?" I say as I sit up and catch it. "It's still warm!"

"There was a pile of them on a cart upstairs. In the kitchen."

"Wait! You've been up into the hotel? Did . . . did anyone see you?"

"There was a man who shouted at me in French," says Violet, taking another bite. "And a fork bounced off the wall behind me as I ran behind a waiter, but I don't think anyone got a good look at me. Why?"

I groan. Monsieur De Grees, the hotel's Belgian chef, guards his kitchen like a fortress. And if he thinks there's a thief around . . .

"Do you know what a cameraluna is?" I ask, taking a cautious bite from my pastry.

Violet shakes her head.

"But you know what a spy is, right?" I say. "Just don't let anyone see you, OK? Things, er, things could get very serious if you do."

"There are spies in the hotel?" Violet's eyes light up.

I ignore the question. I'll be expected to open up my Lost-and-Foundery soon, and already I can hear guests checking in and out at the hotel's reception desk, and the distant sound of breakfast being served.

I start tidying some of the mess from yesterday, and I'm pleased when Violet gets up to help. With the two of us working, it's not long before things are almost back to how they should be in my little cellar: utter chaos, but the sort of chaos where I more or less know where everything is, and where some proper lost-and-foundering can be done if someone rings my bell.

"I wonder where it is," says Violet as we survey our handi-work. "Or where *they* are. They might have had more than one."

"Where what is?" I say, straightening my cap. I'm already struggling to keep up, and the day has barely begun.

"My parents' suitcase," says Violet. "Or cases. I mean, they surely had luggage. Luggage that they would have left behind in the room when they vanished. Well, where is it?"

It's a good question.

I should have thought of it.

"There are hundreds of lost bags and suitcases down here," I say, "going back a century. I'd need to check the register."

"Well, can you?"

"Can I what?"

"Check the register."

I go up to my cubbyhole and lift down the big book where I, and all Lost-and-Founders before me, have recorded everything that has ever been handed in at the Lost-and-Foundery. I bring it down to the cellar, open it out on the floor, and flick back to twelve years before.

"What are the green check marks for?" asks Violet.

"That's for when something is returned to its owner. See, you write a description of the item in black ink, make notes in blue if you have a lead on the owner —"

"If you find clues, you mean," says Violet, but I ignore her.

"And then check the entry off in green if it gets picked up or returned."

"I see. So, is there an entry for Parma? About twelve years ago? I know I was found in December. . . ."

Violet stops talking. I've found the entry, describing two suitcases and several loose items that were handed in the day Violet's parents vanished. The name PARMA is written in careful letters. There are no notes in blue ink and no green check marks. What there are, though, are hard red lines crossing out the entire entry.

"What does that mean?" says Violet.

I fiddle with my cap.

"It means . . . er . . . That is to say . . . the red lines are, um . . ."

"Herbie!"

"Well, I'm afraid it means the owners were declared dead, and the suitcases were handed over to the next of kin. It means your parents' luggage isn't here. It means someone else in your family came to collect it."

Violet shakes her head.

"No. No, that isn't right. My dad has no other family. Except my great-aunt Winniegar, of course."

"Great-Aunt who?"

Violet makes a face.

"Great-Aunt Winniegar. She's my guardian. But she would

never bother with lost suitcases. Not unless she thought there might be cash or jewels in them."

"How do you know there wasn't?"

"Because my dad's a writer," says Violet. "Great-Aunt Winniegar said he wasted his life chasing stories instead of money."

"Not bothered about sentimental value, then, your great-aunt?"

The face again, only worse.

"How about your mum?" I ask. "Didn't she have any family?"

There's a pause.

"Violet?"

But now I cannot see Violet's face at all—it has vanished behind her mass of hair.

"I have no idea who my mum is," she says eventually.

So I go quiet.

Then I see the date.

"Hey, wait, it says here that your parents' cases were collected two years ago. But I was here then! I don't remember that. It's not even my handwriting!"

"Then they must have been stolen," says Violet. "One day, when you were out, someone came here and *took* my parents' things!"

Stolen?

From *my* Lost-and-Foundery!

But it's possible. And if they were stolen, then someone who knows how the Lost-and-Foundery works must have done it.

I go to the shelf where the Parma suitcases should have been, and sure enough, there's a gap. I shove my hand deep into the dark space between the other lost bags. My fingers find something at the back, so I pull it out.

It's two pairs of shoes, all tied together by the laces. Attached to them is a neat label marked PARMA—LOOSE FOOTWEAR. I bring them over and hand them to Violet.

"These belong to you now," I say. "It's all that's left. I—I'm sorry, Violet."

Violet stares at the shoes in her arms, amazed. One pair is a man's brogues, well-worn and scuffed. The other is a pair of lady's boots—stout, ankle-length, and polished smart beneath the dust.

It's the shoes the police found on the harbor wall after Violet's parents went missing.

As I watch, Violet unties the laces with trembling fingers. Then she kicks off the flimsy canvas shoes she arrived in and slips the ankle boots onto her feet.

"Aren't they a bit big?" I ask.

Violet shakes her head.

"My mum must have been quite small."

For a moment I think she's going to hide in her hair again, but she wipes her eyes furiously.

"*IS* quite small, I mean."

Then Violet snatches up the big leather register and taps the page.

"Room 407. It says here that my parents stayed in room 407."

"Well, yes . . ."

"I want to go there," says Violet, shutting the book with a thud. "I want to go there now."

I think about saying no. I think about explaining that sneaking Violet up to the fourth floor without being seen is impossible — not with the chambermaids on their rounds and Mr. Mollusc on the prowl — but one look at Violet is enough to tell me that there's no point.

Somehow or other, we're going to room 407.

⚙

Five minutes later I'm lurking in my cubbyhole, waiting for the coast to clear.

The Grand Nautilus Hotel is a strange place. In high season it's full of summer guests — people in shorts and shades with sunburns, who drift around looking at everything and noticing nothing.

But it's not like that in the winter. In the winter, people stay here only if they have a good reason. Or a bad one. These are the kind of people who look at their reflections in the lobby mirrors just to see if they are being followed. Or ask to be seated where they can see but not be seen. These are people with secrets to keep or secrets to uncover. These are people who notice *everything.*

And that's why I've waited till there's no one at all in the lobby except me and Amber Griss.

The hotel receptionist is standing as usual at her enormous mahogany desk. As I saunter over to her—all casual and nothing's-up-at-all—she makes a face at me that says, "I like you, Herbie Lemon, I always have, but I'm tired of defending you from Mr. Mollusc, so don't try any funny business with me today, OK?"

I have a bit of a reputation.

"Morning, Amber," I say. "There's some funny business going on outside. I think you should go and see for yourself."

"Now, Herbie . . ." Amber warns, peering over her severe spectacles.

"No, really!" I say. "Did you hear that someone stole some croissants from the kitchen this morning?"

"Yes, I did. Chef is furious. . . ."

"Well," I say. "The thief is just outside, selling those croissants around the side of the hotel!"

"What?"

"I can't do anything about it because I'm only twelve-ish, but someone needs to before old Mollusc finds out."

"Old Mo—" Amber starts to say. "I mean, *Mister* Mollusc will go *ballistic* if he finds out. But I can't just leave Reception."

I tug the front of my uniform straight and snap to smart attention.

"I'll cover the desk for a moment," I say. "You can count on me."

Amber looks uncertain.

So I try to look fresh-faced and dependable.

"Fine," Amber says eventually. "Thanks, Herbie. I'll be as quick as I can."

And she leaves her desk and clip-clops across the marble to the great revolving doors, leaving me feeling triumphant and clever and, yes, also a bit guilty.

But I can worry about that later.

I nip behind the reception desk and glance both ways.

Now I'm completely alone.

With the keys to every room in the hotel!

But just as I'm reaching for the key to room 407, something really annoying happens.

There's a *TING* from the elevator. Its doors clack open and Mr. Mollusc steps out.

Of course, he sees me immediately.

"Herbert Lemon!" He spits my name as he strides toward me. "What are *you* doing there? Where's Miss Griss?"

At this point, I could either lower my hand and try a grin, which would almost certainly make me look more suspicious, or I could go for a more daring approach.

I take the key.

"I'm on important Lost-and-Founder business," I say in my poshest voice. "Someone has left something in room 407."

"Sir!" Old Mollusc barks the word out.

"Er . . . sir?" I say.

"On Lost-and-Founder business, *SIR!*" Mollusc corrects, going a little crimson around the edges. "You will address me as 'sir' on all occasions."

"Certainly, sir." I snap to attention again. "Not just on certain occasions, sir, but always, *sir.*"

"Good. Now . . ."

"Sir, sir, sir!"

"What is it?"

"Nothing. Just practicing."

"Just practicing, *SIR!*" Old Mollusc is close to bursting a blood vessel by now. A winter guest, coming out of the dining room, looks over and frowns suspiciously.

"I will, sir. Of course, sir," I say, backing away from behind the desk with little bows, giving the manager enough respect and "sirs!" for him to feel he has won out over me. "Thank you, sir. I must be off now, *sir.*"

And, still clutching the key—and to the sound of Amber clip-clopping back into the lobby—I turn and run up the stairs.

CHAPTER 6

A COIN FOR THE MERMONKEY

When I reach room 407, I'm puffed out. But it doesn't sound like old Mollusc is following me. I turn the key in the lock and push through into the dark beyond.

Room 407 is nothing special. It's the cheapest accommodation the hotel provides. Still, the ceilings are high, and the furniture has a grandness about it, despite being old. In the single tall window, dark-blue velvet curtains hang to the floor, glooming the room. I pull them open and blink in the light.

"Let me in, quick!" says Violet in a muffled voice. She's crouching on the tiny balcony outside. "Anyone could see me here."

I open the window, and she darts inside, followed by a hard-as-nails sea wind.

"Who?" I say. "Who could see you?"

"I don't know," she says, pulling her borrowed coat tight around her and looking fearfully over her shoulder. "Anyone."

I walk out onto the balcony and start polishing the rail with my cuff, as though it's my job. A few people hurry against the wind on the cobbles below. The pier, which stretches out into the sea ahead, is empty. The tide is in, pounding the seawall, and the wind moans around the railings and lampposts, carrying with it a hint of fish and chips from Seegol's Diner. A bank of dark clouds towers on the horizon as if it's just waiting for the right moment to dump a mountain of snow on the old town. I nip back inside.

"I don't think you were seen . . ." I say, but my words trail off as a low moan reaches us from far away, sharpening to a monstrous shrieking roar that rolls around the distant horizon.

"What was that?" says Violet.

I close the window hurriedly and fasten the catch.

"They say it's just the wind."

"They *say* it's just the wind?" asks Violet. "Or it *is* just the wind?"

"I prefer to think it's just the wind." I straighten my cap. "Don't you?"

But Violet doesn't seem to be listening anymore. She is standing in the middle of the room, looking around in wonder. And then I remember that she's been here before.

"I was only a baby. Yet, it feels like . . ."

"Like what?" I say.

"Oh, nothing." She gives me a sheepish grin. "But this is the closest I've been to my . . . to Mum and Dad since . . ."

"Hmm," I say. "But that was twelve years ago. I don't know what you're hoping to find in here now."

"Every time I rehearsed what would happen if I came back to the hotel, Herbie, I imagined there would be luggage. Other things that my parents had left, besides me. I imagined there would be *clues*. Now it looks as if this room might be my only chance to find one."

I shrug. Then I get down on the floor and start poking around under the bed. Anything we find here could have been left by any of the guests who have stayed here since. But Violet must know that already, so I don't see any need to point it out.

After about five minutes of cobwebs and dust, we stop. There's nothing here. For a moment I wonder if we should climb up and look in the small chandelier, but I already know there's nothing there either.

"Did you look in the wardrobe?" I say.

"Twice."

"Well, we should go, then. You'll have to climb back down the fire escape, I'm afraid . . ."

"Climb!" says Violet, snapping her fingers. "Of course! I didn't look *on* the wardrobe."

She grabs the spindly chair from under the tiny desk and pulls it over to the wardrobe. In a moment, she's teetering on top of it in her mother's boots, rummaging around in a cloud of dust of her own making.

"Doesn't anyone ever clean in this hotel?"

"There are hundreds of rooms, you know," I say, "and, anyway, why would anyone clean up there?"

"Because of these," says Violet, and she jumps down from the chair. She is holding a bunch of papers and pieces of card and things, which she spreads out on the bed. There are several receipts, tags that have been cut off vacation clothes, a foreign coin, two playing cards, and . . .

"Aha!" cries Violet, snatching something up in both hands. It's the size of a postcard and has a line of numbers and letters printed on it. Violet cries, "Yes!" and holds it up to me. On the back of the card is a drawing of a crooked little monkey (or is it a chimp?) in a top hat—a monkey with a fish tail.

In a moment, Violet has pulled out the dog-eared card that she keeps on a ribbon around her neck. She holds them both up. They match.

"The numbers and letters are different," I say. "And any one of the guests who've stayed here could have left that card."

"What?" Violet looks unimpressed. "Are you saying it's a coincidence? That two such freaky postcards just happen to be in the same room at the same time, and they're not connected? How can you say that? Unless . . ." She turns on me. "Unless you know something about these cards."

I straighten my cap again and meet her gaze. Almost.

"Herbie! You do know something, don't you? You recognize these weird monkey cards."

"OK, OK, maybe I do," I say a bit mumbly.

"When were you going to tell me?" Violet demands.

And I wonder again why I didn't say something when I first saw the card around Violet's neck. Then I remember it was because I didn't want to encourage this whole detective nonsense, that's why. And yet here I am, the next day, stealing keys and searching for clues and helping a secret girl climb up the fire escape. It's probably about time I just give in and accept that I am on a case now, whether I like it or not.

"It's a prescription card from the Eerie Book Dispensary," I say, throwing my hands up in surrender. "Most people around here have them. It's really nothing unusual."

"Nothing unusual?" Violet is starting to get cross, I can tell. "If it's nothing unusual, why do I have no idea on earth what a . . . a . . . what did you call it?"

"A prescription card," I say. "From the Eerie Book Dispensary."

"Why do I have no idea what that even is?"

"You know how people go to see a doctor to get medicine?" I say. "Well, this is the same, only with books. The stories are like the medicine, see?"

But I can tell from Violet's face that she doesn't.

"You know," I say, scooping up the rubbish from the bed and flicking the coin to Violet. "I think it would be best if I took you there to see for yourself."

CHAPTER 7

THE EERIE BOOK DISPENSARY

It has already started snowing as we head out into the twist-ing streets of Eerie-on-Sea. Only, because this is the seaside in winter, don't go imagining a pretty snow globe flurry. The snow is like a swarm of icy bees—stinging our eyes and trying to get up our noses.

"Is it always as cold as this?" asks Violet, shouting above the wind.

I shrug, though she probably can't tell because of my big coat. And it's not *my* coat, exactly—like Violet, I've borrowed one from the Lost-and-Foundery. All signed out and accounted for in the ledger, of course. In each coat pocket we have a hot pebble from the stack on my stove.

"It's not far," I shout back, and we start to climb a narrow lane of steps, heading deeper into the town.

"Can't see if we're being followed," Violet calls, looking back, "in this weather."

I look back, too, and for a moment it seems as if there is someone there. We both stop, squinting into the snow. Was that a shadow stepping back into a doorway? There are a few people around, hurrying against the wind.

"It's nothing," I say, almost convincing myself. "Mustn't get paranoid."

But I can't stop myself from glancing up at the hotel tower, still visible over the rooftops behind us. Does Lady Kraken's cameraluna work by daylight, too?

We come out into a square with a bronze dolphin statue in its center. We cross it and find ourselves standing outside a large shop window, bathed in its warm light. Something grotesque leers out at us. It's the mermonkey, looking just as ugly as the drawing on the postcard, sitting on a great, peeling circus pedestal and grinning down from behind an ancient black typewriter.

"It's real?" says Violet.

"Well . . ." I shrug. "There's real, and then there's *really* real, isn't there?"

"The Eerie Book Dispensary." Violet reads the painted letters from the window. Then, before she can say anything else, there's a *DING*, and the door of the shop opens.

A tall, handsome man with dark gray-speckled hair steps out and pulls his jacket lapels up against the weather. He stops a moment as he sees us, and pauses. It looks as if he's about to say something, but then he just gives a small nod before striding away across the square.

"Is that the owner?" says Violet. "He looks . . . booky."

"Not exactly," I say. "That was Sebastian Eels. You've probably heard of him. He's an author and a bit of a local celebrity. He's a bit full of himself, too, if you ask me."

"You're not being rude about my customers, are you, Herbie?" says a Scottish voice I know well. A woman with tumbling red hair and a green dress is leaning out of the doorway, pulling a shawl around herself.

"Sorry, Mrs. Hanniver. We were just coming to see you," I say, though I notice Violet is still staring after Sebastian Eels with an odd look on her face.

"Well, come and see me a bit faster, then, and close the door behind you," says Mrs. Hanniver. "It's as cold as Neptune out there."

Inside the shop a cheery fire blazes in a black marble fireplace. We shuffle out of our borrowed coats.

"So, Herbie Lemon. Has someone lost something in my dispensary? And is this, perhaps, the girl who lost it?"

"Not exactly," I say, holding my hands to the fire. "This is Violet. Violet, meet Jenny Hanniver. She owns this place."

Violet says hello, but she's distracted, gazing around the shop in amazement. I remember how it felt to visit the Eerie Book Dispensary for the first time, and to see the sagging floor-to-ceiling shelves—color-coded and stuffed with all manner of books, seemingly in no order at all. I can remember the book I got, too, but that's another story. . . .

"Ah, Violet," says Jenny Hanniver. "I see that Erwin likes you."

I look down and, sure enough, the dispensary's cat, Erwin, is curling himself around Violet's legs. Mrs. Hanniver scoops him up, a mass of snow-white fur and two ice-blue eyes in her arms.

"A good sign. Cats can always tell."

"Tell what?" asks Violet, stroking the cat's head.

But Mrs. Hanniver just smiles.

"Violet's got something to ask you," I say, because the silence is a bit awkward. "Or show you, I mean."

"Oh, yes." Violet reaches into her pullover and pulls the ribbon over her head. "This."

And she hands over her mermonkey card.

"So you've been here before," Jenny says, turning the card in her hand.

Violet shrugs.

"Maybe. My dad's a writer, so perhaps you know him? His name is Peter Parma."

"Peter?" Jenny blinks. "Wait, your name is Violet *Parma*?"

Violet nods. "You . . . you know me?"

"Know you? Not exactly, but I held you in my arms once, when you were a baby. Many years ago."

"You *do* know my parents, then?" Violet's voice goes higher with excitement. "And my mother? You knew my mum?"

"I met her; it's not quite the same thing. Your parents consulted my mermonkey, as many do. And they went missing soon after."

She holds up the card.

"This, I presume, is the book prescription they were given?"

"Must be," I say. "Can you tell which book it was from the code?"

"From the code? No, not a chance." Mrs. Hanniver frowns. "The books change position all the time, as you should know by now, Herbie."

"Hold on." Violet raises her hand. "*I* don't get how this place works. It looks like a shop, but it sounds as though it's something else. What *is* it exactly? A library?"

"The world's one and only book dispensary," Mrs. Hanniver says, handing the card back. "A library will lend you the book you want, while a bookshop sells it for a price. In this place, however, it's the book that chooses you."

"With"—Violet still looks unsure—"the mermonkey? That thing?"

And she points to the grotesque creature sitting in the window. Viewed from behind, its scaly lower body and hunched hairy back are a disturbing sight.

"Why not find out for yourself?" replies Jenny Hanniver.

CHAPTER 8

IN WHICH A BOOK
IS DISPENSED

B ut I don't have any money," says Violet.

She's standing in the shop window now, her back to the glass. In front of her, the mermonkey looks down over the top of its typewriter. Its left arm is extended, and in its hand it is clutching a tall, scraggy, moth-chewed top hat, held out as if asking for an offering.

"You do," I say. "Remember? From your parents' room in the hotel?"

Violet puts her hand in her pocket and pulls out the foreign coin she found on top of the wardrobe.

"It might as well be yours," I say with a shrug.

"But how much does it cost?" asks Violet.

Jenny Hanniver smiles.

"Oh, that depends entirely on you. Some who come here stuff that hat full of cash before the monkey will talk to them. While others have only to brush it with their fingertips. Try your coin, Violet. It's the only way to find out."

Violet reaches out and drops the coin into the hat. It lands with a soft thud somewhere inside.

Nothing happens.

But then, before anyone can speak, something does.

The mermonkey shudders. There's a wheezing, clicking sound like rusty gears being driven by a spring, and its left arm lifts up and up and up, until it plops the hat down on its head. Then there's a rattle as something—the coin, surely—falls down into a hidden mechanism.

The creature's eyes light up.

There's a bone-jarring scream from somewhere, which makes Violet jump in surprise. Steam, or possibly smoke, curls out from the creature's ears as it rises up on its coiled, iridescent fish tail. The mermonkey curls its other arm till its hand stops, hovering over the typewriter. With a terrible screeching sound, it slowly extends a long, bony index finger. Then it starts to type.

"What's it doing?" Violet cries over the horrible, shrieking, clacking sounds. But Jenny Hanniver just nods toward the typewriter.

And then, as suddenly as it started, the mermonkey judders to a halt. Its right hand draws back from the typewriter keys, and the left hand holds the hat out once again. Its eyes wink out, and silence returns to the shop, leaving only a hint of acrid smoke in the air to say that anything happened at all. Then there's a *PING* from the typewriter, and a card is ejected from it, fluttering down to the floor at Violet's feet. She picks it up.

"And that, Violet Parma, is your prescription," says Jenny Hanniver. "It's the book the mermonkey has chosen for you. Not, perhaps, the book you want, or the book you were expecting, but very possibly the book you need."

Violet rejoins us. The card in her hand is just like the one around her neck—a drawing of the mermonkey on one side and a line of letters and numbers on the other:

4 - 2 - E - Pu - 78

"But what does that mean?" she asks. "Is it code?"

"Herbie?" Jenny looks at me with a twinkly eye. "Can you remember how to read mermonkey?"

I scratch my head under my cap.

"Um, I think so. The first number is the floor we should go to?"

Mrs. Hanniver smiles and indicates the stairs, faintly visible deep inside the shop.

"Call me if you need help," she says, and turns away to a pile of books waiting to be sorted on a nearby table.

"Come on," I say to Violet. "This way!"

"And the rest of it?" says Violet as we reach the fourth floor. We're alone up here, with no sound but the creaking of old wood and the wind at the windows. We can see three rooms ahead of us, one after the other, all of them as stuffed to the high ceiling with books as the rest of the place.

"The two means the second room," I say, leading the way.

"And the *E*?" says Violet, when we get there. "Is it . . . East?"

"It is," I say. "And it's easy to orientate in this town—the sea is always the same direction. So this is the east wall. What is the next part of the code?"

"It just says 'Pu.'"

"Pu is for purple," I explain. "See, all the shelves are different colors. Purple's the one-less-than-top shelf."

I grab a library ladder and hook it to the rail on the ceiling.

"There you go, Violet. It's your book; you can have all the fun." Violet climbs.

"The last part of the code is seventy-eight," she calls down.

"That's the book itself," I call back up. "Just count them from left to right. If you get to the end of the shelf before seventy-eight, then count back . . ."

"OK," says Violet, counting under her breath—tapping each

book spine with her fingertip. And then: "I think I've got it."

Violet slides back down the ladder and lands neatly. In her hand is a slim aqua-green hardback book, old-looking and with no dustcover. The title is stamped in faded bronze letters across the cover. It looks as though the last person who read it used a piece of dried seaweed as a bookmark.

"So this is mine?" she asks, clearly still unsure about all this. "My book?"

"In more ways than one, perhaps," says a man's voice, and we nearly jump with fright. A shadow crosses the next room, and Sebastian Eels fills the doorway. He pushes one hand through his thick hair, and a few half-melted snowflakes flutter down. "Now, that is a *very* interesting choice."

And he takes the book.

"*Malamander*," he reads the title out, "by Captain K. So mysterious, isn't it, when an author tries to hide his real identity? But it seems the mermonkey has chosen to tell you a story about our famous local legend, Violet. The tragic story of old Captain K and his battle with a monster."

Violet reaches out and takes the book back. Politely, but quite firmly.

"How do you know my name?"

"So sorry—rude of me. Jenny just told me who you are. Peter Parma's girl. I'm Eels, by the way. Sebastian Eels." And he holds one large slablike hand out to shake. Violet's hand is engulfed by it. "I dabble in a little writing myself."

"We should be going," I say, heading toward the doorway.

There's a pause before Sebastian Eels moves out of the way and allows us through.

"Of course. Well, goodbye, Violet. If you ever need any help with that book, feel free to get in touch. I'm something of an expert on the legend of the malamander. And you can often find me here."

We are just heading back downstairs when the author calls out to us.

"Oh, and I would be especially interested to hear if you catch sight of it yourself."

Violet stops and looks back.

"The malamander? I thought you said it was just a legend?"

"Oh, indeed." Sebastian Eels grins, passing his tongue over his teeth as he does so. "But in a place like Eerie-on-Sea, legends can sometimes have a little more . . . bite."

CHAPTER 9

COPROLITES AND CUTTLEFISH

H e's just trying to wind you up," I say to Violet as we leave the book dispensary and step back out into the cold. "Sebastian Eels likes to have an effect on people. Just ignore him."

"He gives me the creeps," says Violet. "Why did he leave the bookshop and then come back in again?"

"He's a writer, isn't he? Can't stay away, I expect."

"Well, for some reason he seems especially interested in my book," says Violet, patting her coat pocket where she's slipped the slim green volume.

"We should get back." I turn up my collar. "It's getting colder, and I'd like to fire up my stove. I need to open the Lost-and-Foundery again before Mr. Mollusc gets ideas and decides to board it up for good."

"I don't want to go back to your cellar," says Violet. "Not yet, anyway. I want to look at the sea."

"Er, really?" I say, glancing up at the slate-gray sky and getting a fat snowflake in the eye.

"And I want you to tell me about this malamander thing."

"OK, OK," I say. "But let's not hang around here."

When we reach the seawall, it has at least stopped snowing. We look out over the beach, which has appeared again now that the tide is retreating. To one side, the pier stretches out into the ocean, its iron understructure emerging from the heaving waves. Seegol's Diner is the only point of light to be seen on it.

"Hungry?" I say to Violet.

"Yes. But now I really don't have any money."

"My treat," I say. "Come on, let's go down to the beach first. I know a shortcut."

The narrow stone steps to the shore are wet, and slimy with green. When we reach the sand, it's odd to think that just a couple of hours ago the place we are now standing was over our heads with water.

"Are you paid, then?" asks Violet as we set off across the wet sand and shingle. "For your lost-property job?"

"Oh, yes." I straighten my cap, which the wind keeps pushing over one ear. "But not in money. Being the Lost-and-Founder at the Grand Nautilus is more important than that. I get to keep anything that is not collected."

"Really? Anything?"

"Yes. Well, anything that is not collected after a century."

"A hundred years!" Violet looks amazed.

"I know! At least once a week something gets signed out of the ledger for good. If no one has collected it after a century, they're probably dead and gone, aren't they?"

We crunch on through the shingle, picking our way over the seaweed piles and sticks of driftwood. Ahead someone well-wrapped in tatty coats and scarves is approaching, carrying a metal bucket. On her head are at least three hats, all tied down with a piece of string.

"Halloo!" the someone cries, and I "Halloo!" back.

"I don't often see you on the beach, young Herbie," says the woman as she draws near. "Who is your interesting friend?"

"This is Violet," I say. "Violet, this is Mrs. Fossil. She's a beachcomber."

"*Professional* beachcomber, if you please," says Mrs. Fossil, giving Violet a snaggletoothed grin. "The only one in town. And I hope to see you both in my little Flotsamporium in the near future. I have some curious beach finds, just in and cleaned up.

They would especially suit a young man looking for something for that special someone in his life. Eh, Herbie?"

Mrs. Fossil nudges me and winks at Violet.

"Really?" Violet looks embarrassed. "What kinds of things do you find?"

"Ah, things like this," says Mrs. Fossil, waving her bucket at Violet. Inside, a dozen strange objects—shells, twists of metal, frosty glass pebbles, and funny spirals—slosh around. Mrs. Fossil reaches a fingerless glove into the bucket and pulls out a glistening brown lump.

"What's that?" asks Violet, not taking the lump, even though it looks as if Mrs. Fossil is offering it to her.

"Coprolite, my dear. A lovely specimen. Prehistoric."

"Copro . . . what?"

"Doodah," explains Mrs. Fossil, with another wink. "Dino turd. Petrified poo! One hundred thirty-five million years old, give or take a day or two. I'm probably the first person to pick it up since the Lower Cretaceous. Imagine that!"

Violet, whose hand had been hesitantly reaching for the brown rock, looks as though she can imagine that only too well, and she thrusts her hand firmly back inside her pocket.

"Or maybe you'd prefer some sunglasses," Mrs. Fossil continues, dipping back into the bucket and pulling out a pair of shades. They've obviously been in the sea a long time. At least, if the barnacles on the lenses are anything to go by. "Clean up a treat, these will."

"Not just now, thanks, Mrs. F," I say, pulling Violet away. "But we'll come around to your shop sometime soon, I promise."

"Just you see that you do!" Mrs. Fossil calls back as she strikes off across the beach again, back hunched, eyes fixed firmly on the ground.

Soon we are approaching the end of the pier that is out of the sea. As it looms over us, dripping from its seaweedy struts, I see the metal spiral staircase that I was looking for rising up from the beach and connecting to an open hatchway in the wooden boards of the pier high above us.

"It's not exactly a secret way," I say to Violet as I signal for her to go up first, "but hardly anyone uses it these days."

I don't tell her that another interesting feature of the staircase is that no one can see it from the town. Not even if they have such a thing as a cameraluna to spy with.

At the top, we emerge under a little ornate shelter encrusted with Victorian curlicues. From here we can see along the pier to the glow of warm light that spills from the windows of Seegol's Diner.

"It's the best fish and chip shop in town," I tell Violet, leading her toward the light. "Well, it's the only fish and chip shop in town. But it's still really good."

"Isn't this a funny place for it?" says Violet. "On the pier?"

"It is a bit far from everyone, I suppose. Especially if you have to fight a gale force nine to get here. But people come anyway. And if they want to see Seegol they have to."

"What do you mean?"

"Seegol never leaves the pier. Ever. He's lived here, alone, for years."

CHAPTER 10

SEEGOL'S DINER

I dig my hand into my pocket and scatter its treasures across the table.

Seegol gives me one of his sideways eyebrow looks and scratches his stubbly head. Then he turns to Violet.

"It's always the same with this one." He waves his hand at me. "Now he'll tell me these things are valuable."

"But they are valuable." I poke around in the pile of curios and trinkets. "This coin here is solid silver."

"Ah, but my fried fish is *golden*," says Seegol.

"So is this earring," I say back, and I slide it over so he can get a better look. "These things are old, Seegol. Some of them really old. They were lost in the hotel more than a hundred years ago."

Seegol picks up the earring, holds it to the light, and scrutinizes it closely. Then he lets a grin spread across his face and slides it back across the table.

"He always tells me that, too," he says to Violet. "And he always convinces me."

He scoops up the silver coin and pushes the rest back to me.

"Fish and chips for two, coming right up."

It's hot in Seegol's Diner, but after the cold outside, that's welcome. We've shuffled off our coats and settled down by a window. In fact, the whole place is windows, with the kitchen an island of scrubbed metal in the middle. There are a few locals

here, chatting over steaming plates and drinking tea or coffee. You can tell they are locals because they don't flinch like Violet does every time the diner shudders.

"What's doing that?" she says, clutching the table as another rumble of motion passes through the building, making the plates and cups rattle.

"Waves," I explain. "We're on a pier, remember."

"Aren't you worried it'll collapse or something?"

I shrug.

"It's never done that before. And Seegol lives here, in a flat above the diner. He must think it's safe."

"What's the story with him?" Violet hunches forward so her words won't carry. "Seegol. Where's he from?"

"I've never actually asked," I say, surprising myself as I realize this. "I don't recognize his accent. They say he came here as a young man and saw a mermaid from the end of the pier. Heard her sing. No one ever recovers from that. He's been waiting for her to come back ever since."

"Another legend?" says Violet. "There seem to be a lot of those around here."

Outside the weather has begun to change. The dark clouds have been replaced by a strange blue-gray light. Through the windows, all details of the sea and the town become fuzzy and indistinct as the wind dies and a sea mist creeps in.

"Seegol's coming back," I say under my breath. "Quick, get your book out."

"What for?" Violet looks confused.

"You want to find out about the malamander, don't you? Trust me, leave the book on the table and see what happens."

"Two plates of crispy golden fish and chips," Seegol announces, arriving at our table and placing the food under our noses. The salty, vinegary smell of the chips makes it suddenly hard to think straight.

"Thank you, Mr. Seegol," says Violet, putting her book down in a very obvious place and eating a chip. Then another and another. "Wow, these are amazing!"

"Ah!" Seegol sighs, giving a little bow. "Always a pleasure to . . ."

And that's when he sees the book.

"This?" he says to Violet, lowering his voice and glancing over his shoulder. "You are reading this?"

"Yes. Well, sort of. I just got it. I don't really know what it's about."

"It is about the fish man," says Seegol, whispering now. "But it is not something to talk about here. My customers, they get scared. It is not real. That is what I tell people. It is better that way."

"You make it sound as if you aren't so sure," says Violet. "About the malaman—"

"Shh!"

Seegol sits down quickly at the table, nudging it with his fat belly as he does so.

"Please, do not say its name."

He picks up the book and pushes it back into Violet's hands before continuing.

"You are right. I am not so sure. It is not possible, of course, for there to be a scaly creature that can walk like a man and swim like a fish. Yet, I have seen things. On the pier, at night, in the shadows, I have seen things. In my country, we leave gifts for beings like this, for spirits. Offerings. At night, when I close up, I, too, leave gifts — the fried fish that is left over — outside on the pier. In the morning, it is gone. And so, I have never had any trouble."

"Seagulls might have something to do with that," I say, and Seegol raises both shoulders in a shrug.

"I have no trouble from the seagulls either. Maybe it is all the same thing."

"But what have you seen?" says Violet, breaking off a piece of battered fish. "In the shadows. What is this thing supposed to be?"

But before Seegol can answer, there's a loud creak and a rush of cold air as the door of the diner swings open. A tall, dismal figure stands there. He has a lank bone-white beard and a long

black sailor's coat, dripping with water. I slide low in my seat and lean on my hand, hiding my face. Violet sees me, looks over at the newcomer, and shrinks back into her hair.

"Boat Hook Man!"

"What are we going to do?"

The trinkets and other objects from my pocket are still on the table. I push the gold earring over toward Seegol again and hope that the expression on my face speaks clearly enough.

Seegol looks from me to Violet. He ignores the earring and gets to his feet.

"It is good to see you again, sir," Seegol calls over to Boat Hook Man. "Please, have this seat, with the best sea view."

And with that he steers the awful man away from us and over to the opposite side of the diner. He won't be able to see us from there.

"Good old Seegol," I whisper, gathering up my things. "But we should go."

"No, let's wait," says Violet, popping another chip into her mouth. "This might be our best chance to find out just who Boat Hook Man really is. Maybe he's meeting someone here."

It's a good plan. And perhaps it would have worked. But just then something happens that changes everything.

Outside, where the sea mist is gathering, someone screams.

CHAPTER 11

THE SIGHTING

B oat Hook Man is the first to his feet, standing so abruptly that his table crashes over. Then he crosses the diner, flings the door open, and lumbers out.

The scream comes again.

"Come on!" Violet cries, pulling me out of my chair.

Everyone else gets up too, and we're able to hide in the small crowd that rushes out onto the deck of the pier to see what's happened. We lean over the side, our eyes straining in the swirling mist.

"What's that?" someone shouts. "Look, there!"

Down below, where the beach is barely visible, a human shape moves into view, stumbling out of the mist.

Boat Hook Man lets out a strange sound, like the moan of a distant wind, and turns, heading straight for the hidden spiral staircase down to the beach. As he goes he lets his right arm drop by his side, his long, hooked spike dangling like a weapon.

"What's he going to do?" Violet whispers in my ear. But I don't know, do I? I look back down at the figure below, and the figure looks up. I recognize the face immediately.

"Mrs. Fossil!" I shout, waving. "Helloooo! What happened?"

But Mrs. Fossil seems unable to speak. Her face is contorted with fear or pain, or both. One of her hats has fallen off.

"We need to get down there," Violet says, and sets off at a run in the same direction as Boat Hook Man, who has vanished now into the mist.

I follow and find myself rattling down the spiral staircase faster than is wise, but I'm more concerned about getting down quickly than I am about not slipping. We jump the last few steps and run back down the beach beneath the dripping pier.

"Mrs. Fossil!"

"Oh! Oh, Herbie!" comes her voice. "Help me!"

The sea mist is so thick now that if we didn't have the struts of the pier to follow, we'd struggle to know which way was which.

Mrs. Fossil is on her knees in the sand, clutching one arm and sobbing with pain.

"It hurts! Stings!"

"What happened?" Violet crouches down beside her. "Did you cut yourself?"

The sleeve of Mrs. Fossil's raincoat is torn to shreds, as are the many layers of clothing below that. There are angry red marks on her skin.

"It bit me!" she cries. "I saw it! Oh, Herbie, I saw it. Teeth like needles!"

"It's OK, Mrs. F," I say. "We'll get you back to town and call the doctor."

I place my shoulder under her arm, and Violet does the same. We manage to raise her to her feet.

"But I saw it!" Mrs. Fossil wails. "I saw it!"

"What did you see?" Violet says through a grunt of effort. "What bit you?"

"The mala . . . the mal . . ." Mrs. Fossil tries to say it, but her teeth seem to be locking together. Then her legs give way, and suddenly we're the only things holding her up.

"We need," I gasp, "to get her off the beach . . ."

But I trail off, because something is moving ahead, between us and the town. Something dark and immense. Something that is getting closer.

Boat Hook Man steps out of the mist. His eyes lock on to Violet. He raises his hook and points it at her. His mouth opens—a black cavern in his scraggy beard—and he bellows in a voice like a distant gale.

"I find you!"

"Please," says Violet. "We need help. We need to get this lady to a doctor."

Boat Hook Man doesn't seem to hear. He stomps forward, and with his one good hand he grabs Violet by her collar, lifting her in the air.

"You . . . cannot stop us!" he gusts. "I will . . . be free!"

"Hey!" I shout, staggering now under the unshared weight of Mrs. Fossil. "Leave her alone!"

But there's nothing I can do. Mrs. Fossil is passing out, taking me down with her.

Then there's a *SLAP* from behind us—muffled by the mist, but quite definitely a slap. It sounds like something large and flippery hitting the wet sand. Then it comes again. We all turn, even Boat Hook Man.

Something is in the mist, in the direction of the sea, too far away to be clear. It's a crouching figure, hunched low near the water, as if poised, waiting to spring. But there's something funny about it, something odd about the length of its arms, something fishlike and spiny that keeps this from being a some-*one* at all, and more like a some*thing*.

Where its eyes should be, there are two enormous pale

reflectors. They blink, twice. Then it moves off — darting from its crouch and springing along the murky foreshore at great speed, its feet *slap, slap, slapping* as it vanishes in a swirl of mist.

Boat Hook Man drops Violet, his eyes wide, his mouth drawn back to bare his teeth. He sets off at a lumbering run, vanishing into the mist after the strange figure.

"Are you OK?" I ask Violet, struggling to my feet and extending my hand to pull her up. Mrs. Fossil is sprawled at our feet, out cold.

"I think so," Violet croaks, clutching her throat.

More figures emerge from the mist now, this time from the direction of the pier and the town.

"She's here! Over here!"

It's Seegol. He reaches our side, with several of the other customers from the diner.

With a heave, four of them manage to lift Mrs. Fossil, and they set off up the beach toward the town.

"I will telephone the doctor," Seegol calls back to us, jogging off toward the pier steps. "You should follow the others."

"Yeah," I say, fishing my Lost-and-Founder's cap out of a pool of seawater and wringing it out. "We need to get out of here."

"Wait a moment," says Violet. "What just happened? Herbie, what was that we saw by the water?"

"You wanted to know about the malamander, didn't you?" I reply. "Well, I'd say Eerie-on-Sea has just obliged you with your very own sighting."

"But it can't be real." Violet shakes her head. "How can it be real?"

"Do you see that?" I say, pointing into the mist.

"What?"

"Exactly. Violet, in this fog, anything could be standing ten paces away *right now*, and we wouldn't know. We need to get off the beach. It's dangerous here."

"OK," says Violet. "Maybe you're right. But there's something we need to find first." And she heads off into the mist where Mrs. Fossil's footprints are still faintly visible in the waterlogged sand.

"What are you doing?" I say, trying to catch up. "This is madness. What do we need to find?"

"That!" Violet cries, pointing ahead.

Something is lying on the beach, on the edge of visibility. Violet jogs over to it and picks it up. It's Mrs. Fossil's bucket, her beachcombing treasures spread out around it.

From where I'm standing, Violet is half vanished in the mist. I see her silhouette as she stoops to scoop the spilled things back into the bucket.

And then I see something else.

A shape. No, *the* shape. The strange, crouching, spiny shape from a moment ago, faint but massive in the mist beyond Violet. And it's getting closer, making a throaty, clicking, burbling sound as it comes.

"Violet, behind you!"

This time she doesn't hesitate. It must be the panicky high-pitched squeak in my voice, which, for once, is actually quite useful.

Then we are both running up the beach, not looking back — running and running until we reach the top of the steps in the seawall, and we can see the town and the cheery lights and the door of the Grand Nautilus Hotel.

CHAPTER 12

EXOTIC ERRATICS

When I get back to my cubbyhole, Mr. Mollusc is standing there.

"Where have you . . . ?" he begins. Then he notices the too-big borrowed coat, my seaweedy trousers, and the fact that my Lost-and-Founder's cap is a soggy mess on my head. And I'm still carrying Mrs. Fossil's bucket of stinking beach findings, which is dribbling a trail of seawater on the polished marble floor behind me.

The vein on his temple starts to throb.

"What . . . ? How in . . . ? *Why* . . . ?"

"Have you lost a question, sir?" I say, sliding past him.

I flip the sign on my counter from CLOSED to PLEASE RING FOR ASSISTANCE.

"I'll just pop downstairs to see if someone has handed one in."

Then I descend to my cellar, leaving the hotel manager spluttering behind me.

Violet has already climbed in through the window and is sitting in my big armchair.

"What just happened, Herbie?" she says.

I scratch my head. As is often the case in Eerie-on-Sea, that's not a question that's easy to answer. I take my coat off and drape it over a chair beside my stove. Fortunately, a small glow is still winking at us in the stove window.

"First thing is to get warm and dry," I say, chucking in a couple of logs. "The legends and monsters can wait."

"I don't believe in the malamander," says Violet. "I don't know what we saw just now, but I'm not ready to believe in sea monsters. Yet, what *did* we see?"

I wring out my cap into Mrs. F's bucket.

"We saw a shadow in the mist, that's all. And Boat Hook Man attacked you."

Violet shudders. "Do you think he attacked poor Mrs. Fossil, too?"

"He looks as if he's capable of anything," I say. "But one

thing is sure, he seems to have a thing about you. And what did he mean by 'I will be free!'?"

Violet pulls a blanket over to the chair and wraps herself in it, staring into the window of the wood burner, where a new flame is just flickering to life.

"Violet?" I say, because her silence seems a bit odd. "Surely you must have some idea why he's chasing you? What did you do?"

She shrugs.

"I just bumped into him. Yesterday, when I arrived in town. That's all."

Can that really be all? But with someone as freaky as Boat Hook Man, maybe there are no good reasons for anything.

Violet is watching me from under the blanket.

"I came here to find my parents, Herbie," she says. "But I seem to have found a different mystery instead."

I rummage around in my clothes box until I find another Lost-and-Founder's cap.

"Unless the two mysteries are connected somehow," I say.

Violet frowns at me.

"How can they be connected?"

I'm about to reply, "Of course they must be connected!" when there's a sharp, scratchy sound on the window. We both turn. Something white is pawing at the glass.

"Ah, it's only Erwin," I say, getting up to let the cat in. "He often visits. Especially if he's caught in bad weather."

"The cat from the Eerie Book Dispensary?" says Violet. Erwin hears her voice and pads over to her. He lets her stroke him for a moment before jumping up onto a shelf above the wood burner and settling down in a pile of lost scarves.

"Where I got the book," Violet continues, as if to herself. "Where I got the book about the malamander. I only went there because of the card around my neck — the card from my parents that came from the dispensary. Oh, Herbie, maybe these things *are* connected."

Violet reaches across to her drying coat and fishes the slim green book out of the pocket.

"But how?"

"The best way to find out what's in a book is to read it," says Erwin.

"She hasn't had a chance yet," I reply absentmindedly, brushing the last of the sand from my trousers. "But you'll have time now, Vi. I need to get some work done, or Mollusc will have me stewed and served up as today's special. I'll be back soon, though, to see what you've found out."

Violet is holding the book to her face, her wide eyes staring over it at Erwin.

"That . . . that cat just *spoke*!"

I glance sharply at Erwin. He peers back through narrow blue eyes, as if challenging me.

I give an awkward shrug.

"Maybe your ears are still full of sea mist," I manage to say. "Everyone knows cats can't talk."

And I give Erwin a hard stare, which he ignores as he purrs down to sleep.

"Anyway, now would be a good time to read your book, Vi," I say as I head for the stairs. "And when I get back, maybe you'll have some answers."

⚙

Back up in my cubbyhole, I look both ways to make sure there's no sign of Mr. Mollusc in Reception. When I see that there isn't, I stroll over to Amber Griss again. And, again, she watches my approach over her spectacles.

"Herbie," she says, "If you're going to tell me you've seen the croissant thief again . . ."

"No," I say. "Not a sign. But I'll keep my eyes open, I promise."

"What have you done to get Mr. Mollusc so worked up today?" asks Amber. "He is fuming."

"I'm just returning these." I put the keys to room 407 on the counter. "They were lost and I, er, I found them. It's my job, after all. I don't know what old Mollusc breath is on about."

"Now, now," says Amber, suppressing a laugh as she takes

the keys. Then she adds, "I wonder how these got lost."

I give her one of my most innocent faces.

"Who knows? Anyway, as part of my official duties as Lost-and-Founder, I need to look at the booking records," I say, adjusting my cap and trying to look important. "I need to trace some guests."

"I see." Amber raises one eyebrow. "Do you know which room they stayed in?"

"Room 407, as it happens," I reply, checking my fingernails.

"Really?" The eyebrow creeps even higher. "What a coincidence."

Amber takes a large volume down from a shelf behind her and opens it on the counter.

"They stayed here twelve years ago," I say. "Maybe it would be better if I had a look?"

Amber stops flicking pages and gives me another over-the-spectacles glance. Then she turns the book around and pushes it over. It takes only a moment to find the entry for Violet's missing parents, marked with the single word "Parma."

Violet's dad's name was Peter Parma. But Violet seems to know nothing at all about her mum—not even her name.

"Is there some way to find out more?" I ask Amber.

"People don't need to give their shoe size to book a room here, Herbie," she replies.

"But what about this phone number?" I say, tapping a column on the opposite page.

"We always take a phone number, for every booking. This looks like a London number. Why . . . ?"

"Amber, it's really vitally important that I use the hotel telephone."

Amber Griss puts her hands on her hips.

"Can you look me in the eye, Herbie Lemon, and swear that you're not doing anything else to annoy Mr. Mollusc?"

I put my hand over my heart.

"Amber, I swear to you, on my honor as Lost-and-Founder,

that I will never, *ever*, pass up the chance to annoy that whiny old whinge-bag Mollusc. And I think you already know that."

Amber laughs and points to the old black and brass telephone.

"Just one call. I'll keep a lookout for the whinge-bag."

I pick up the heavy receiver and dial the number from the booking record. I hear the purr of the phone ringing, and then a voice answers.

"Exotic Erratics. What name, please?"

"Um . . ." I say, because I wasn't actually expecting an answer, let alone one as strange as this.

"Ah, good morning," says the voice, sounding slightly more formal now. "You're through to the Natural History Museum, Department of Cryptozoology and Exotic Erratics. How may I help you?"

"My name is Herbert Lemon," I say slowly, putting on the posh voice because, well, because *Natural History Museum!* "I am the Lost-and-Founder at the Grand Nautilus Hotel, and I am calling because I believe you have lost something? Or, rather, *someone?*"

"Who is this?" The voice sounds annoyed now. "How did you get this number?"

"This would have been twelve years ago," I continue before they can hang up. "Did someone in your department go missing?"

I hear a faint intake of breath on the other end of the line.

Then the voice tells me a name.

CHAPTER 13

MRS. FOSSIL'S
BUCKET

It's the next day, and a frosty sun is climbing above the horizon. When I get up, Violet is already awake and staring out of the cellar window at the ankles of the people passing by. Upstairs in the hotel is the suitcase clatter of guests in Reception.

"Did you sleep well?" I ask.

Violet has built some kind of nest for herself, behind the coatracks where a hot-water pipe runs along the wall. She was already asleep down there when I got back the evening before, and this is the first time I've seen her since.

"Yes. After reading for a bit."

"I don't suppose you stole any more pastries from the kitchen," I say.

Violet shakes her head. "You told me not to, remember?"

"I get a plate of stale ones every morning," I explain. "Chef used to save me freshly baked, but . . . well, Mr. Mollusc put a stop to that when he found out. I'll bring it down here and we can chew over what to do next. Oh, and I've found something out."

When I get back with the rubbery croissants, Violet is sitting in the armchair, the still-damp contents of Mrs. Fossil's bucket spread out on a suitcase in front of her.

"Herbie, can you remember where Mrs. Fossil was hurt?"

"Under the pier," I say.

"No." Violet rolls her eyes. "I mean, where on her body? It looked like her hand and arm. Is that right?"

"I think so." I sit on the floor beside the suitcase. "Are you thinking that maybe one of these things might have hurt her? When she picked it up?"

There are dozens of objects. One is a silver fork, corrosion-eaten and strange-looking after years in the sea, but not sharp.

"I don't think any of these things could have drawn blood," Violet says, pushing them around with her finger. "It's just funny pebbles, weirdly shaped driftwood, shells, and bits. And I think this is an ammonite."

"What's that, though?" I say, pointing to an oddly translucent red stone, about the size and shape of a very large egg.

Violet picks it up and walks over to the window. She holds the stone up. It gathers up the morning light and seems to hold it inside itself, glowing in Violet's palm like a small red sun.

"Whoa!" I say.

"It's pretty," Violet replies, tossing the stone in her hand. "But hardly dangerous. I think it's a big lump of sea glass, that's all."

"Nice bit, though," I say. "Mrs. F has loads of that stuff in her shop. She'll want it back, I expect. I'll take it around later."

"Let's both go," says Violet, sweeping the things back into the bucket. "I want to see how she is, anyway. And I need to find out more about what we saw yesterday, on the beach."

⚙⬤✿

Mrs. Fossil's Flotsamporium is in a different part of town from the Eerie Book Dispensary, but the twisting narrow lanes and tall seaside houses look the same. The ground floor is mostly an enormous bay window, filled with jars and bottles. In the glass of the peeling shop door, the word CLOSED is displayed, painted on a piece of driftwood.

I knock anyway.

After a moment the door opens, but the person who looks out isn't Mrs. Fossil.

"Dr. Thalassi," I say. "We've come to see your patient."

"I cannot advise it," says the man, his dark brows lowering over his Julius Caesar nose. "Mrs. Fossil has had a nasty shock. She needs to rest —"

"Is that Herbie Lemon?" comes Mrs. F's voice, a bit wobbly, from somewhere deep inside the shop. "And his friend Violet? Oh, please let them in, Doc. They were on the beach with me yesterday."

We enter, and I hear Violet gasp as she takes in the extraordinary interior of the Flotsamporium. The bottles and jars in the window — backlit now by the morning sun — burn and sparkle with translucent pebbles of every imaginable color. Violet looks down and sees her own body dappled with rainbow light.

"Sea glass!" says Mrs. F, also noticing Violet's wondering expression. "Mermaid's tears! Broken bottle bits, thrown away as rubbish, rolled by the sea for countless tides, turned to jewels by the power of nature."

Mrs. Fossil is sitting in a rickety folding beach chair, surrounded by teetering mountains of beachcomber finds. There are more glass jars of minerals, tide-rolled pieces of china, shells of every possible shape and pattern. There are petrified dinosaur

bones piled next to lost frog-
man flippers, fishermen's
floats, and children's plastic toys by the basket. Nets
hang from the ceiling like
the webs of giant sea spi-
ders, and over everything
floats the scent of tea and
toast, and the mysterious
faraway tang of the ocean.

"Come in!" Mrs. Fossil
waves us over. "I would boil
the kettle, but . . ." And she
indicates her right hand.

Mrs. Fossil's arm is laid
out on a makeshift table
made from half a surf-
board and a plastic drum.
Her sleeve is rolled back to
reveal, across her hand and
wrist, a curve of angry red
wounds.

"That must really hurt,"
says Violet.

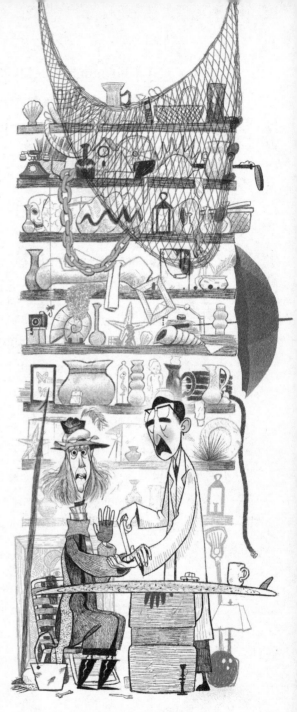

"It's just a bit numb today," says Mrs. F, though one look at her pained expression suggests that it actually hurts a great deal. "And I can already move my fingers again. Doc says I'll be right as rain in a jiffy."

"If by 'jiffy' you mean a week, then maybe," says Dr. Thalassi. "You are lucky I didn't have to call an ambulance yesterday."

"What did this, Doc?" I say, pointing at the horrible wounds.

Dr. Thalassi waggles his great black eyebrows until the specs on his forehead fall down onto his beaky nose. He leans over Mrs. F's arm.

"When I first saw this, I thought it was a jellyfish sting. See how the red marks are strung out in a line? But closer inspection reveals puncture marks. There is no doubt; this is a bite. The bite of a large venomous creature."

"I didn't know we had creatures like that here," I say, glancing at Violet.

"We don't," says the doctor, pushing his glasses back up to his forehead.

"But we do in stories," says Mrs. Fossil in a quiet voice. "We have the malamander."

"What did you see, Mrs. Fossil?" asks Violet. "When this happened? What can you remember?"

Mrs. Fossil goes pale. Or paler than she is already.

"Teeth," she whispers. "Teeth like needles. It came out of a rock pool beside me as I was admiring something I'd found. I had no time to react. . . ."

"You mustn't get agitated," says the doc, beginning to bind her arm. "It only accelerates the poison around your system. Please try to relax."

"We found your bucket," Violet tells her, holding it up. "I tried to pick up everything that had fallen out."

"Thank you, my dear."

"I wonder," says Violet, tipping the contents onto the surfboard. "Which of these things were you holding in your hand when the . . . whatever it was . . . bit you?"

"Well, do you know, I think it was that nice piece of red." Mrs. Fossil nods toward the fiery stone we were admiring earlier. "The sea glass. It's quite a beauty, isn't it? A rare color."

Dr. Thalassi finishes binding up Mrs. F's hand and wrist, and he snaps his medical bag shut.

"Oh, thank you, Doc," says Mrs. Fossil. "I don't know what I'd have done without you. Why don't you help yourself to something? For your museum? A little thank-you gift from my beachcombing treasures. I found some lovely coprolites yesterday. I know how much you like your dino poo."

"Museum?" asks Violet.

"I am, in fact, not only a medical doctor," says Dr. Thalassi. "I am also a doctor of natural history. I curate the local museum here in Eerie-on-Sea."

"Herbie, haven't you taken your friend to see it yet?" Mrs. Fossil says. "The museum is one of the sights!"

As the doctor heads for the door, he stops and turns.

"Are you serious about making a contribution to the museum?" he asks Mrs. Fossil.

"Of course! Without you I'd be languishing in a hospital bed somewhere, pumped full of goodness-knows-what. Help yourself."

"Then I select this," the doctor says. He returns to the surfboard table and picks up the large piece of red sea glass. He holds it up to get a closer look, and ruby light seems to shine out of it, tinting his olive skin with a strange glow.

"Really?" Mrs. Fossil looks confused. "Wouldn't you prefer something ancient? I have an Iguanodon thumb spike over there that's much better than the one you have on display in the museum. Wouldn't you rather have that?"

"It's kind of you, but I have set my heart on this trinket," says Dr. Thalassi, slipping the red stone into his jacket pocket. "And now, I really would urge you to rest, Mrs. Fossil. I will return tomorrow, to change your bandages."

And with that, he opens the door of the shop and leaves.

CHAPTER 14

WHAT A BEACHCOMBER KNOWS

So, do you really think you've been attacked by the mala-mander, Mrs. F?" I say, settling down on an upturned fishing crate beside her.

"Oh, Herbie, I really don't know," says Mrs. Fossil, wincing as she tries to move her bandaged arm. "I always said I believed in the old stories, but honestly, I was just saying that to amuse people. You know, the tourists we get in the summer? This is our Loch Ness Monster, after all. They come in the shop and ask if I've seen anything. So, of course, I tell them yes—glimpses in the sea mist, that sort of thing. It makes them more inclined to buy something. I never actually took the legend that seriously, but now . . ."

"What is the malamander legend, exactly?" says Violet. "I mean, the one everyone knows. The one the tourists ask you about."

"Oh, there are lots of different stories about it, going way back," says Mrs. F. "It's a monstrous creature—half man, half fish, half goodness-knows-what—that has haunted these misty shores since before ever a town was built on Eerie Rock. They say it can sometimes be glimpsed as Midwinter approaches, as it searches for somewhere to lay its magical egg."

"Magical egg?" says Violet. "What kind of magical egg?"

"Oh, the grants-you-your-dearest-wish kind." Mrs. F chuckles, with a return to her usual cheerfulness. "The whole makes-your-dreams-come-true shebang! But, of course, you only get that if you can take the egg. And to take the egg, you have to defeat the malamander."

"Which no one can do," I throw in, remembering the first time I heard the tales too. "On account of its hideous spikes and steely scales and it being, you know, a monster."

"So what happens to it, then? The egg?"

"The creature devours it," says Mrs. Fossil. "As the sun rises the next day, when its mate never comes, it eats up that egg and slinks back into the depths for another year."

"But have people tried to take it?" says Violet after a

thoughtful pause. "I mean, in the stories. Have people tried to steal this amazing wishing egg?"

"Oh, endlessly!" Mrs. Fossil chuckles again. "Heroes galore in the legends. Every single one of them"—she rolls her eyes and waggles the fingers of her good hand in a way she probably thinks is spooky—"gobbled up by the beastie!"

Violet doesn't smile.

"Anyway," Mrs. Fossil continues, "the tourists love it. Gives them something to look out for when the mists come in and they try a bit of beachcombing for themselves. Everyone loves a good story."

"But you'd never actually seen anything yourself?" asks Violet. "Before yesterday?"

"Oh, I wouldn't go *that* far. You don't spend hours on the foreshore in all weathers without having strange experiences. Or hearing strange sounds. Those mists in particular can addle your senses, make close things seem far away and far away things seem . . ."

"Close enough to nearly bite your hand off?" I say, finishing the sentence for her.

Mrs. F grimaces and begins to look exhausted.

"I really don't know what I saw, my dears. And that's the truth of it."

"There could be a plain and everyday explanation for it all, I suppose," says Violet. But she doesn't sound too sure. She glances again at the door through which Dr. Thalassi just left.

"Is sea glass valuable?" she adds, turning back to Mrs. F. "I mean, more valuable than a genuine dinosaur bone?"

"Oh, don't mind old Thalassi," says Mrs. Fossil, managing a weak smile. "He'd never admit it, but his museum and my shop are more or less the same thing. He'll have that old lump of red glass on a pedestal by the end of the day. With a fancy label on it, no doubt. You should go along there and see for yourself."

⚙O✿

We leave Mrs. Fossil to her shop and her bandages and head back out into the narrow street. It's midday, and almost sunny, but there's still a hard nip in the air, and I want to get back to my cubbyhole. But Violet isn't having any of it.

"I won't find any answers there," she says. "I think we need to go back to the beach."

"You're not scared?" I say. "After yesterday?"

"There's no mist today," says Violet. "Why, are *you* scared?"

"Of course not." I straighten my cap nervously. "Not a bit."

"Then let's get down there," says Violet, pulling her coat close around her and leading the way.

"I was surprised you asked so many questions about the legend," I say, running to keep up. "Back in Mrs. Fossil's shop. I thought you were reading about it in the book the mermonkey gave you."

"Herbie," says Vi, coming to a halt. "Have *you* ever read that book?"

"Um," I say, fiddling with my buttons. "Not in so many words. . . ."

"So you haven't read the description of the magic egg?" asks Violet. "The malamander egg that can grant wishes?"

"Er . . ."

"So you don't actually know what it looks like?" says Violet.

"Does it . . . ?" I squint, scratching my head beneath my cap. "Does it look like an egg?"

Violet is unimpressed. She turns and marches off toward the beach, with me flapping along behind.

We come out through an old stone archway onto the seawall, which in this part of town is actually fortified ramparts. Ahead of us the beach stretches away for miles, the tide low and the sea only a distant murmur. Directly below us are the spindly fishermen's sheds—painted black, with seagull-dropping roofs. Reaching up between them are the spikes of stone that jut from the sand like giant teeth, giving them their name: Maw Rocks.

Violet leans out over the wall and takes a deep breath of freezing sea air. Then she turns to me.

"It's not just an egg, Herbie. Like the kind you can make an omelet with. The malamander egg is described in the book as being a wondrous ruby red. Red, Herbie! With a glow inside like fire. A red glowing egg made of something like crystal."

"You mean," I say, "like the thing Mrs. Fossil was picking up when she was attacked?"

"Exactly," says Violet. "Like the thing your Dr. Thalassi has just taken away in his pocket."

CHAPTER 15

BOAT HOOKS

The steps down to the beach from the ramparts are narrow and sea-smashed, giving way to raw rock in places. The lower ones are almost completely covered in seaweed, but we manage to get down in one piece.

"What are these?" asks Violet, pointing to the towering black sheds.

"Fishermen's huts," I say. "Most of them haven't been used for years, but some of the fishermen still keep their tackle here."

Between two of the huts, each several stories tall, an old rope fishing net has been hung, like a cobweb set to catch seagulls.

"That's how they dry them," I explain. "The nets, I mean. Hey, Violet . . ."

I pick up the pace, because Violet has turned a corner, ducked beneath the net, and vanished.

When I catch up to her, she's trying one of the shed doors.

"You can't just go in there," I say. "These fishermen are hard men. Sea-hardened, you know? You don't want them catching you messing with their stuff."

"There's no one here now, though, is there?" she replies, pulling the door open with a creak. "I'm just taking a look."

I follow her inside — well, I have to, don't I? It's dark in the shed, but in the small light that creeps in, I see a ladder bolted to the inside of the wall. And I watch Violet's feet as she disappears up it.

"I thought you wanted to go down the beach," I whisper-hiss up the ladder as I follow. "What are we doing in here?"

"I want to see the view" comes the reply.

We reach the top story, which is black and airless and smells like fish guts. The only light comes from the edges of a tall hatch in the wall. Violet fiddles with the catch and then shoves it open. The rush of fresh air that floods in is a relief.

The beach is laid out before us, with the pier and the far sea directly ahead.

"You'd get a better view from the seawall," I say.

"I know," says Violet, leaning out of the hatch and looking

each way. "But on the seawall, everyone can see me. Here is more private."

"What is it you want to do?" I say.

"Isn't it obvious?" says Violet. "Something is happening in this town. And whatever it is, it's happening on the beach. I want to watch it for a while."

She pulls out her book.

"I can finish reading this at the same time."

"I admit, it's a good view," I say, looking out of the hatchway at the gleaming expanse of sand. "You can even see the *Leviathan* from here."

"The what?"

"Over on the horizon, where the waves are now. Do you see it?"

Violet leans out.

"I can see something dark and jagged. It looks massive. What is it?"

"It's all that's left of the battleship *Leviathan*," I tell her. "It was wrecked years ago. You can walk out to it when the tide is at its lowest, though it's pretty dangerous. And some say . . ."

I trail off.

"What?" says Violet, but all I can do is point.

I hear Violet gasp.

"Boat Hook Man!"

It's true. And he's not over by the pier or stalking across the horizon by the wreck. He's *right below us*, shuffling zombie-like between two of the sheds, his head swinging from side to side, as if he's looking for something.

"Get in," I whisper, pulling Violet back inside the shadow.

"What's he doing here?" she whispers back. "Was he following us?"

I say a bad word. Not a *really* bad word, but bad enough. After everything that's happened, we should have been more careful.

We creep forward again and crouch in the shadow of the hatchway to watch. Boat Hook Man stops and cocks his head, as if listening. We go completely still. He cocks his head the other way.

And then he looks down.

Down at the wet sand where two sets of footprints are clearly visible. Footprints that lead straight to the door of the shed we are hiding in.

Boat Hook Man looks up, and we dart back again.

"Oh, bladderwracks!" I say. "He saw us. He's coming up!"

And sure enough, the ladder that is bolted to the inside of the shed—which rises up the entire four stories—starts shaking violently.

"Which means we can't go down," says Violet. "So . . ."

She runs to the hatchway and grabs a rope that is attached to a small pulley outside. For a moment I think Violet is going to rappel down, which would be nuts, as the rope is nowhere near long enough. But I'm wrong. Instead, while I'm standing there like a lemon, clutching my cap, Violet *swings out into midair*!

The ancient building creaks and cracks under the strain.

Violet lets go of the rope at just the right moment and grabs the hanging net — the one spread between two of the sheds. The net sags under her weight, and the building complains again, but Violet gains her balance and is now safely outside. The rope swings back toward me.

"Quick, Herbie. Jump!"

Well, you've probably worked out by now that I'm not a "Quick, Herbie, jump!" kind of guy. I mean, it's not as if there's much need for jumping and exclamation marks in the daily life of a lost-property attendant. But Violet has changed all that. Also changing it is the dismal bearded face of Boat Hook Man as he rises up through the floor behind me, streaming with water. He slams his hook into a beam and pulls himself up into the room in one easy motion.

So I jump out of the hatchway and grab the rope. Well, what else can I do?

I swing out. . . .

But I've got the angle all wrong.

I miss the net and swing straight back toward the hatchway!

"Herbie!" Violet shouts, making her way across the net toward me.

Boat Hook Man grabs the rope with his good hand, just above my head. And now I'm dangling, four stories up, like a fish on a line. The boat hook comes up and draws level with my eyes.

At this point, I can let go of the rope and probably break both my legs, or I can stay dangling where I am and be filleted like a small lemon-flavored herring in a Lost-and-Founder's cap.

And that's when something blue-green flashes in front of my face. Something blue-green and angular, which strikes Boat Hook Man in the eye.

It's Violet's book.

Boat Hook Man staggers back, his mouth open in a wordless cry of shock, his good hand clutching at his eye.

And no longer holding the rope.

"Herbie!" Violet shouts again, but I don't need to be told this time. I kick hard and push myself away from the shed, swinging out in the right direction. I throw myself forward and just about manage to get a hand on the net. Violet grabs my coat and pulls me up beside her.

The two rickety black sheds creak ominously as the net swings under our weight.

We begin to climb down, but it's slower than you might imagine, because the net is so loose. We're only halfway down

when everything shudders, causing us to lose our grip . . . and fall. We grab on again and look up to see that Boat Hook Man has jumped, too—that was the shudder we felt—and is now in the net above, hanging by his hook, staring down at us with a face like a thundercloud, seawater showering from his swinging beard.

"Let go, Herbie!" Violet cries, and she does so herself. We're still quite high, and I hear her land heavily on the sand beneath me. I let go, too, and land beside her, the air escaping from my lungs with an "OOF."

Violet starts to run but cries out and falls down again. "My ankle. I've hurt it."

"Hold on to my arm," I say, snatching up my cap and getting ready for us to run as fast as we can together. I risk a glance back and I'm pleased to see that it's not easy to climb down a loose fishing net when one of your hands is a boat hook; Boat Hook Man looks hopelessly tangled.

But we don't get to start that run.

"Well, well, well," says a voice as the broad frame of a man appears between the black sheds ahead of us, barring our way to freedom.

"This is no way to treat a book," the man adds, picking Violet's green book up and brushing the wet sand off it.

It's Sebastian Eels.

THE MALAMANDER EGG

....

I think the mermonkey meant for you to *read* this," says Sebastian Eels, handing the book back to Violet. "Not to use it as a Frisbee."

"We need to go," I say, helping Violet up and preparing to lead her away, but stopping because the man moves back in front of us. Up above we can hear Boathook Man continue in his struggle down the net.

"Or could it be," Eels continues, "that you have read it already and don't like what you found?"

Eels is looking intently at Violet, as if searching for some sign. Behind us we hear a wet thud as Boat Hook Man finally reaches the sand. I turn and see him hulking toward us, his hook held high. I'm just about to yell at Violet to run, never mind her bad ankle, when Sebastian Eels holds up his hand to Boat Hook Man.

"Now, now, my friend. No need to get excited. I told you, I just wanted to chat with these young people, not terrify them. And that hook of yours is very intimidating. They must be worried about what an angry man like you could do with such a fearsome weapon."

Boat Hook Man comes to a halt, just a few paces away from us.

"It is . . ." he says, in a rush of damp air, "it is the girl . . ."

But Sebastian Eels silences him with a look.

"Chat?" says Violet, dropping my arm and standing as tall as she can. "Chat about what?"

Sebastian Eels is still watching Violet closely. His eyes flick to me for a moment and then back to Violet.

"Oh, I think we just got off to a bad start, that's all," he says with a smile that is obviously meant to be charming. "Back in the book dispensary."

Then he turns to Boat Hook Man and says in a commanding tone, "Stay here. Rest awhile. Come to me again later."

I risk a glance over my shoulder. Boat Hook Man hesitates a moment and then begins to back off, receding into the gloom between the sheds until there's nothing to be seen there but a strange patch of swirling mist.

"I'll walk you back to the town, Miss Parma," says Eels, putting his arm around Violet's shoulders. "I doubt you can move very fast with that hurt leg."

"I'll be fine, thanks" comes Violet's cold reply as she ducks out from under the man's arm.

"Oh, I'm sure you will," Eels says. "It must have been hard for you to grow up without your parents. It's impressive that you have decided to come here looking for them. All by yourself. That is, you *are* here all by yourself, aren't you? In your searches? Apart from the gallant Herbie, naturally."

"What do you mean by that?" asks Violet.

"Well, I'm just wondering if you are working with someone. To find your parents, I mean. The, er, police, for example? Or perhaps some form of private detective agency?"

"I have Herbie," says Violet, setting off at a limp. I groan inside as I follow. "It's his job to get lost things back home again. He's the only detective I need. Unless there's something *you* can tell me about my parents?"

"Me?" Eels says, catching up with her. "Oh, I don't think I can help you. I only wish I could. I'm just an old daydreamer, that's me. Like all writers, I suppose. I'm only here for the stories."

"Like the story of the malamander?" says Violet.

"It's true that that particular legend has long fascinated me,"

Eels says, adjusting his tie. "It's a complex tale with ancient roots."

"In that case," says Violet, "you must know all about the malamander egg."

At that, I swear, Sebastian Eels twitches, ever so slightly. He recovers and gives Violet a sideways look.

"So, you're curious about that," he says. "A magical egg that can grant your wishes? That can make your dreams come true? Like the sound of it, do you?"

"Wouldn't anyone?" says Violet in a neutral voice, and I realize what she's doing. She's fishing for information by pretending to know more than she does.

"And if you had such a thing in your possession, Violet Parma," Eels continues, "if you could wish for your heart's desire, I wonder what you would choose."

Violet doesn't say anything. And frankly, I'm not surprised.

"Your poor lost parents, of course." Sebastian Eels supplies an answer for her, with an exaggerated sigh of sympathy.

Violet still doesn't speak. I look at her, but it's hard to see her face now, inside her hair.

"What a shame such magic doesn't exist," Eels goes on, kicking a small pebble across the beach. "That all we have are stories."

"You don't believe in any of it, then?" says Violet. "You don't believe the malamander is real?"

"Goodness me, no!" Eels chuckles. "We folklorists have to keep a level head. Stories like this often perform a social function. In this case, generations of worried parents have used the mala- mander as a bogeyman to scare their children away from the sea. The beach at low tide can be very dangerous."

"And the roaring, wailing sound?" I say. "That you can sometimes hear from the sea? People say that's the malamander calling for its long-lost mate."

"People will say anything for a bit of attention," says Eels, with a superior smile. "But it's just the wind howling around the wreck of the old battleship. Nothing mysterious about that."

"What did my dad think? I won- der." Violet stares straight ahead as she asks this.

"Oh, dear Peter," Eels replies, with a shake of the head. "He had some fanciful notions. He could have been a great man if . . . Well, it's too late now, isn't it? Such a tragedy he died so young."

"My parents aren't dead," says Violet firmly. "Only missing."

Sebastian Eels says nothing.

"What, er, notions?" I ask, because I really don't like these awkward pauses.

"Well, I don't mind admitting that Peter and I didn't always see eye to eye," says Eels, "but his conclusions about the malamander were especially . . . *comical.* He actually seemed to believe that the creature was real! It's probably just as well he didn't finish his book. If it had been published, it would have been a great embarrassment for him."

"Wait! My dad was writing about the malamander, too?" says Violet.

Eels turns to look at her sharply. If I had to guess, I'd say Violet has just revealed how little she really knows.

"Indeed," he says.

"And you've read it?" says Violet. "My dad's book?"

Sebastian Eels pauses, as if measuring up how to respond.

"I read some of the manuscript, yes. But it was never finished, and sadly, all Peter's papers have gone missing, too. Such a shame."

We reach the steps back up to the town.

"Well, goodbye, Violet Parma," says Eels, lifting his hat. "I would rest that leg for a few days, if I were you." He begins to turn away but suddenly swings back.

"Oh, but if you should come across any of your dear father's writings, I would be prepared to offer a reasonable price for them."

"You'd buy my dad's unpublished book?" says Violet. "I thought you said it was 'comical.'"

"I'd still like to preserve his work." Eels smiles. "For old times' sake." Then he fixes Violet with a narrow eye. "I'd pay handsomely for even a single page . . . should you find one."

And with another tip of his hat, Sebastian Eels turns and strides away across the beach.

CHAPTER 17

JENNY HANNIVER

"Blast this stupid leg!" Violet groans, flopping down on a bench on the promenade. The climb has obviously been hard on Violet's sprained ankle. I look back down to the beach, but there is no sign of Sebastian Eels now.

"Sea mist coming in again," I say. "It's going to get even colder, Vi. Whatever else Eels said, he's right that you should rest that leg. Let's get back to my Lost-and-Foundery. I can share my leftover lunch with you."

"And then what?" says Violet, rubbing her ankle. "We don't seem to be getting anywhere."

"At least we know that Boat Hook Man and Eel Face are working together. And the things he told you, about the malamander . . ."

"Herbie, I came here to find my parents, not a monster."

"But what do you want to do, then?" I say.

Violet looks up at me.

"It's time I got some straight answers."

She gets to her feet and starts limping into town.

"I want to see the only other person I've found who actually met my mum and dad."

❀❂❀

By the time we reach the Eerie Book Dispensary, the sea mist has engulfed the whole town. The streets are already emptying as everyone hurries home. It's so cold now that everything the mist touches gains a sparkle of ice.

"Looks like she closed early," I say, rattling the door. "Jenny Hanniver doesn't keep regular hours anyway. We should go before we freeze to death."

Violet bangs on the door.

"Hello?" she shouts through the mail slot.

Some people walking on the other side of the square glance over, curious.

Inside the window, just visible in the cold winter light, the mermonkey grins down at us from behind its enormous black typewriter.

"Seriously, Vi," I say, lowering my voice, "there's no one in."

But then, Erwin the cat is there.

One moment there is nothing but fog; the next, the cat is curling around Violet's legs and purring ferociously. Violet stoops to pick him up, her hands vanishing into his thick white coat of fur.

"He must have crept up on us out of the mist," I say. "Poor thing wants to get in. Where can Jenny be?"

"I'm here," says a voice, and we turn, squinting into the gloom. Jenny Hanniver steps out of the mist, wearing a long, scale-patterned coat and a furry green scarf. When I catch sight of her face, I think for a moment that she looks tense—worried, even. But then she smiles, so perhaps not. It's hard to tell anything straight with this mist.

"I'm not actually open, as you can see," Jenny says as she fiddles with an enormous bunch of keys. "But since you seem to be rescuing my cat, the least I can do is let you in and warm you up."

Inside, the embers of a fire glow in the grate. I think to myself that it's odd of Jenny to go out and leave a fire burning unattended in a book dispensary. Was she called out urgently? Or am I trying too hard to play the detective?

"You closed early?" I ask as Jenny throws logs on the fire.

"Sea mist days are never busy," she replies. "And besides, I had to visit the doctor."

"Dr. Thalassi?" says Violet, limping into one of the fireside armchairs.

"Yes," says Jenny, removing her coat and scarf and looking at Violet. "And maybe you should see him, too. How did you hurt your leg, Violet?"

"I—I just twisted it."

Jenny pulls over a low stool and lifts Violet's leg onto it.

"Let me get you a hot drink and then I'll take a look. A tight bandage should help you move more easily." She walks to the door but then turns to look back at Violet. "I was wondering when I'd see you again."

"Does she seem a bit funny to you?" I whisper to Violet after Jenny has gone. "A bit . . . shifty?"

"She said she went to see Dr. Thalassi," Violet whispers back, "but she doesn't seem unwell to me."

I shrug. You can't always tell if someone's ill just by looking at them.

When Jenny comes back, she has a plate of biscuits and three mugs of hot chocolate. She puts the tray on a low table between us and asks Violet to take off her boot. It's not until she's wrapping Violet's ankle in a soft white bandage that she speaks again.

"So, Violet Parma, did you read the book the mermonkey chose for you?"

I glance over to the mermonkey, sitting hunched and hairy

in the shadows, its back turned to us. In the flickering light of the fire, with nothing but dusk and freezing mist in the window beyond, it almost seems to be moving.

Violet fishes the book out from her coat pocket and props it open near the fire.

"It, er, got a bit wet today," she says. "But I've started reading it, yes."

"And?"

"And I'd like you to tell me," says Vi, "how well you really knew my dad."

Jenny doesn't answer as she finishes the bandage. Then she sits back with a sigh.

"I wanted to say something yesterday. But when I saw which book you'd been given, I thought I might be interfering."

"Interfering?" Violet blinks. "That's a funny thing to say. Interfering with what?"

"It's the same book your parents were dispensed, Violet," Jenny says. "That last night before they disappeared."

Violet picks up the book again and stares at it, openmouthed.

"The truth is, I knew your dad well," Jenny continues. "That old mermonkey must have dispensed dozens of books to him over the years. In fact, it's probably because of Peter that it's still working at all."

"Really?" says Violet.

Jenny gives a rueful smile.

"The mermonkey used to break down a lot, so I took to getting in new parts to mend the mechanism. Peter put a stop to that. He said I had to fix the original part, no matter how twisted the lever or how worn the gear. He once even stopped me from changing its tatty old hat for a new one. He said the magic wouldn't work if I changed a single thing. So he patched that old hat up himself, and it's still there to this day. And so is the magic."

Jenny gets to her feet and walks over to the shop counter, behind which are hundreds of clippings, postcards, and pictures. She pulls something off the wall and comes back to hand it to Violet.

"Your father often stayed here for weeks at a time," says Jenny. "There are spare rooms upstairs, and I'm happy to put people up, especially if they've come a long way to consult the mermonkey. Peter was here a great deal at one time, because of his work."

I lean over and see that Violet is holding a photograph. It shows a scholarly looking black man with large glasses and a close-cropped beard. He looks serious, but somehow playful at the same time, as if he were snapped just at the moment he was about to break into a smile.

Violet is staring at the photo with bright eyes. It doesn't look as though she can speak right now.

"You can keep the photo, of course," says Jenny.

Then I spoil the moment by making a rude slurping noise with my cocoa.

"When you say his 'work,'" I blurt out quickly, "do you mean his writing?"

Jenny nods.

"Peter Parma was a brilliant folklorist who loved our old legends. One legend in particular."

"The malamander," Violet says. She opens her book and slips the photo inside.

"I don't think anyone in the world knew more about that story than Peter," Jenny says. "He was obsessed with it, by the end."

"I've met another writer who calls himself that." Violet brushes the last of the sand from the cover of her book. "An expert on the malamander, I mean. And that's Sebastian Eels."

Jenny pokes the fire.

"He knew my dad, too, didn't he?" Violet says.

Jenny stares at the poker in her hand for a moment. Then she shoves it onto the wood scuttle.

"Oh, yes," she says. "They knew each other, all right."

CHAPTER 18

THE MONSTER HUNT

Your dad believed that the malamander is real," says Jenny, warming her hands on her mug and staring into the fire. "Sebastian Eels did not. That's really where the trouble began."

"Why did he believe it?" asks Violet. "Did he see something?"

"Yes," says Jenny. "He would go out on the beach at night, at low tide, and walk in the moonlight. He swore blind that he saw things scuttling from shadow to shadow or creeping along the sands, just at the edge of sight. One misty night he came back here, banged on my door at some crazy hour, gabbling about seeing the malamander. I liked him, so I didn't mind. Everyone in this town has a story to tell about the foreshore on winter nights. It's that kind of place. But Peter was sure he was onto something—something new. He was writing a book, a huge book. The definitive work on the subject, that's what he called it. He said he was going to put the malamander on the map. He said he was going to solve the mystery of it once and for all. But he didn't reckon on having competition."

"Eels," I say, and Jenny nods.

"Sebastian Eels was also writing a book. He'd been working on what was supposed to be the greatest work on the malamander for years, since long before Peter showed up. Looking back, I suppose it was inevitable they would clash. You see, while your dad came to believe passionately that the creature was real, Sebastian knew with equal certainty that the malamander was just a story, a myth—a cautionary tale told over centuries to frighten children."

"So what happened?" asks Violet.

"They went hunting for it," says Jenny. "Simple as that. After months of arguing and confronting each other, your dad said they should settle the matter once and for all and go out together to look for it. If they found the monster, Sebastian would have to agree to abandon his book."

"But," I say, "what if they didn't find it? Would Vi's dad have stopped writing *his* book? That doesn't seem fair. Not finding something doesn't prove it isn't there."

"I know," says Jenny, "but Peter was so sure of himself that he was willing to risk it. That was the deal they made. So one winter's night, out on the beach, at a low tide of Peter's choosing, they went monster hunting together."

"And did they find anything?" says Violet.

"No one knows for sure what happened. They set out at ten p.m., with nothing but rain gear, flashlights, and cameras. The next day, early, a small crowd had gathered on the seawall to watch them return. The whole town knew about the expedition. I was there myself. When the men came off the beach, they looked terrible. They were covered in silt and sand, and their hair was wild. Neither one would speak, and to my knowledge, the two never exchanged a single word again. Your father came straight here, to his room, packed, and left town."

"But what did they see?" Violet says, her eyes as wide as scallop shells. *"What happened?"*

Jenny shrugs. "Nobody knows. Except Sebastian. If you really want to know, you'll have to ask him. Most of the town thought they'd just had a fight and that was that. All I can tell you is that after your dad left, Sebastian Eels stopped working on his book. Just abandoned it. It looks as though there won't be any great work on the malamander after all."

"But wait," says Vi, with a frown. "When did this happen? This wasn't when my dad vanished, was it?"

"Oh, no," says Jenny. "Exactly one year after all this happened your dad came back. It was Midwinter, and he just turned up at the door, all smiles, as if no time had passed at all. He had the manuscript of his book under his arm—a huge pile of papers, all finished and ready to be published, or so he said. And he wasn't alone. He had a woman with him, and you, Violet—a tiny baby, barely a few months old."

"A woman?" asks Violet. "My mum?"

"Yes," says Jenny. "I hadn't met her before, but I always got the feeling your dad had someone. That was the only time I met her though."

"What's her name?" Violet's voice is so small now we can hardly hear her. "My mum. What's her name?"

Jenny shakes her head.

"I'm really sorry, Violet. I can't remember. It was a very brief meeting, and I was just amazed to see your dad again. He wanted to show your mother the mermonkey, I think. Took its hat and put it on, playing the fool. He was in high spirits. I got to hold you a moment, while this was going on."

"But surely you can remember something about her," says Violet. "What was she like?"

"All I remember," says Jenny, "is that she was—how can I put it?—sciency. Seemed to belong to a different world from your dad, I mean. He was all dreams and wild ideas, while she was more . . . sciency."

I nearly drop my mug.

"Exotic Erratics!" I cry.

Violet and Jenny look at me in amazement.

"Oh, bladderwracks!" I say. "I'm such a ninny! Vi, I completely forgot to tell you! I found something out. I found out who your mother is."

And I tell them about my phone call.

"*The* Natural History Museum?" Jenny gives me a disbelieving look. "Herbie, are you sure?"

"I swear it's true. That's what the man said."

"But what's this about 'Exotic Erratics'?"

"Well, that's what he said when he answered the phone. Then when he heard it was a stranger on the line, he changed it to something longer. Something about a crypto and a zoo . . ."

"What name did he give you?" Violet cries, looking as if she's about to jump up and shake me. "Herbie, my mother's name!"

"Bronwyn," I declare, remembering. "Bronwyn Strand. *Doctor* Bronwyn Strand, actually."

"Yes, that sounds right!" says Jenny. "Now that you say it, it rings a bell."

"Bronwyn," says Vi, slumping back. "My mum."

There's quiet then, apart from the crackling of the fire. Erwin returns and jumps onto Violet's lap. She strokes him absently, but her eyes remain fixed on her mother's boots as they dry beside the fire.

"*That* was the last I saw of your father, Violet," says Jenny. "The next morning I heard that a baby—you—had been discovered alone in a room at the Grand Nautilus Hotel and that your parents had vanished. There were tracks down by the sea, and two pairs of shoes were found. One of the fishermen reported a missing boat. No one knows what happened to them, even to this day."

CHAPTER 19

CLOSE ENCOUNTER

I bet Sebastian Eels knows," says Violet as the door of the Eerie Book Dispensary closes behind us.

It's properly dark now, and getting late, but the mist seems to be lifting, and the moon cuts through the haze above us. Our footsteps crackle in the frost as we pass the dolphin fountain and leave the square.

"I bet he knows exactly what happened to my mum and dad."

"You could be right," I reply. "But what can we do about it? We can't confront him without any evidence."

"How much do you trust Jenny?" Violet asks, and I look at her in surprise.

"I've never thought about it, but I don't see why she'd lie to us. Why do you ask?"

"I don't know," says Violet. "It's just that I wanted to ask her a question, but suddenly thought I should keep it back."

"What question?"

"About the malamander egg," says Violet.

"It seems to me," I say as we start down the narrow steps toward the hotel, "that if you want to know more about that part of the legend you should read the rest of that book of yours. When we're safely back in my cellar and not freezing our cockles off out here, you can have another good go at it, Vi, and maybe find the answers for yourself."

"Yeah, maybe . . ." says Violet. Above us the last of the sea mist melts from the sky, and we stop and gaze in wonder at the inky blackness of space, sparkling with stars.

"What's that?" asks Violet.

"The inky blackness of space," I say. "Sparkling with stars."

"No, not that. *That!*"

I look where she is pointing. Just above the rooftops, one star burns brighter than the rest, fierce and red. As we watch, the light dims till it's almost out before flaring bright and red again.

"That's no star," says Violet.

I'm about to say something when a sound cuts through the

night air. It's a screeching, roaring wail, and when it dies down I find I'm clinging on to Violet, and she's clinging on to me.

"OK, and what's *THAT*?" Violet says.

"Close," I reply. "That's what that is. *Too* close."

As our eyes adjust to the moonlight, we see that the strange, pulsating red star-that-isn't-a-star isn't in the sky at all, but in a window. The window of an old tower, above the battlements.

"That's the museum," I say.

"Dr. Thalassi's museum?"

Just then the terrible, shrieking wail comes again, echoing in the narrow street, and the red light winks out altogether. For a moment, as we watch, a dark and spiny shape seems to scuttle up the wall of the tower, but when I blink to make sure I'm not seeing things, it disappears.

"We should go," I say, trying not to squeak.

"We certainly should," says Violet, "before we miss something important."

And she hurries off toward the museum.

"Wait!" I grab her coat. "I didn't mean *that* way. I meant back to the hotel."

"But the adventure is that way"—Violet pulls herself free—"not back in the hotel."

"But back in the hotel there aren't any strange lights or terrible nightmare sounds!" I squawk, flapping my arms.

"Curiosity may have killed the cat, but that doesn't mean cats shouldn't be curious."

"Ha!" I cry. "That's easy for you to say."

"Except . . ." Violet replies, blinking. "Except I didn't say it. *He* did."

I look to where she's nodding. Erwin is sitting on a nearby window ledge, giving us both a significant look.

"Seriously?" I say to him.

But the cat just purrs and licks his paw like any other cat in the world. And by the time I turn back to Violet, she's already running off into the dark, toward the museum.

So there's nothing left for me to do but run after her.

I catch up to her as she's heading down another flight of steps and out into a dimly lit street. From here I can see Mrs. Fossil's Flotsamporium. There is a light on somewhere inside, and I wonder how she's doing, but I can't stop to knock now—Violet is off again. It's only when we come out onto the battlements, at the fortified western end of town, that Violet finally comes to a halt. She crouches in a shadow and nods across the expanse of cobbles to a crenellated medieval building that hulks on the other side.

"Is this it?" she whispers.

"Yes, the museum is in the old castle," I whisper back. "Well, the doctor's office takes up some of the ground floor part, but all that up there is the museum, including the tower."

Violet looks up at the tall gothic windows. They look back at us, black and vacant. Silence is over everything, and I begin to wonder if we really saw or heard anything strange at all. Unsurprisingly, at this late hour, the tall arched door of the museum is firmly shut.

"Where does that go?" says Violet. She's pointing at a flight of ancient steps that wind up around the back of the building.

"Side way in," I reply. "But—"

Violet darts out into the moonlight and crosses to the castle. Then she trots up the steps and vanishes from view.

"What are you doing?" I say in my loudest whisper. "Violet!"

I find her standing on the top step, beside a gnarly wooden door. Of course, she's testing the handle.

"Seriously, Vi, it won't be open. We should go."

Violet releases the door handle with a sigh.

"After all that, we've missed it," she says. "Whatever 'it' was."

From the steps we can see over the highest part of the town's ramparts, down to the shore far below. The sea mist, which has by now entirely seeped out of the town, is collecting on the beach below us. With the moonlight pouring down, it looks like a rolling ocean of silvery vapor, making it impossible to see what may or may not be on the sand below.

"Do you have a flashlight?" says Violet. "I just want to peek through the window." When she sees the expression on my face, she adds, "And then we'll go, Herbie. I promise."

I rummage in the enormous pocket of my coat and pull out a small flashlight. I join Violet at a window beside the door, place the business end of the flashlight right against the glass—to avoid reflection—and click it on. Inside the museum, dark shapes and twisted shadows are thrown into relief by the sudden light.

"Happy now?" I whisper.

Violet squints in, shielding her eyes.

"I can't see much."

"Which is why we should come back tomorrow when the museum is actually open," I say, and I shut off the light.

But Violet suddenly gasps, and she grabs at the flashlight in my hand. It's an unexpected movement, and the flashlight falls and hits the hard flagstone with a *crack*.

"What are you doing?" I say, but Violet ducks down and pulls me after her.

"There's something in there!" she hisses in my ear.

"It's a museum," I say. "Of course there's something in there."

"Something *moving*." Violet puts her finger to her lips.

Slowly, we both rise up and peer into the window.

Nothing.

Just dark, and blackness, and nothing. But then . . .

. . . two pale orbs, side by side, blink at us with reflected moonlight.

I say that bad word again. I can't help it. If those are eyes, they are the size of grapefruits!

Then something hits the glass. A flat, flippery *something* that slaps the window right in front of us with such force that it shatters. We fall back, shards of glass and window frame raining down all around. I feel points of pain on my hands and face as the pieces cut in.

Then something huge is there, slipping through the shattered window—a fast-moving shadow that blots out the moonlight above. It jumps over our heads, hitting the rampart wall with a clatter. It begins to throw itself over the edge.

Except it can't.

Violet is jerked to her feet by some tremendous force. I see that she is going hands first, and I realize why: she is holding on to something!

Is it a tentacle? Or a tail? Or just a piece of hose? In the gloom there is no way I can tell. All I can see is that if Violet doesn't let go, she'll be pulled over the ramparts too, down onto the toothlike steeples of Maw Rocks, far below.

So I grab her by the boot and am dragged hard against the wall.

"Let go!" I want to shout, but I can't, not with the air being crushed out of my lungs. I struggle up and seize her coat with my other hand and pull back as hard as I can. From here, I can look down the wall. Violet is now halfway over the rampart, her hair dangling crazily over her face, her fists still tightly balled as she clings to . . . whatever it is!

The two orbs of light flash again. There's a shrieking howl, and something swipes across my field of vision. Is it a hand? Is it a claw or a flipper?

Violet cries out in pain and finally lets go, and we both fall back onto the steps. The dark shape of what could be a tail whips away, and I jump up to the wall, desperate to get a good look at it whatever it was attached to.

I expect to hear a thud, and maybe the crunch of breaking bone, as the tail-owner falls and hits the rocks. But instead there's just a faint flippery sound, then nothing. A shadow flits between two spurs of rock, vanishing in a swirl of mist. There's a hint of movement in the fog farther down the beach, and then even that is gone. Soon all we can hear is the faint washing of the tide as the invisible sea creeps slowly back up the land.

DR. THALASSI

When I found out who you were, Violet Parma, I thought your arrival might mean trouble for this town. But I never thought vandalism would be the problem. Why on earth are you breaking windows in my museum?"

We're sitting in Dr. Thalassi's study, behind tall glass windows that look out over the main hall of the museum. From here, the exhibits beyond are nothing but strange skeleton shapes. The only light comes from a paraffin lamp that hisses on the desk. The doctor had this with him when he found us crouching in shock on the ramparts. The folded umbrella he brandished as a weapon is on the desk, too, like a polite threat.

"It wasn't me," protests Violet. "I didn't break anything. It was . . ."

"I'm listening," says the doctor, one thick black eyebrow raised at us.

Violet looks at me. I shrug back. After all, what *did* we see?

I clear my throat and hope that the Band-Aids on my face don't look too ridiculous.

"As official Lost-and-Founder at the Grand Nautilus Hotel, I assure you that neither I nor my associate here would break your windows for fun, Dr. Thalassi—"

"You can drop the posh voice, Herbie," interrupts the doc, lowering both eyebrows into a single monster caterpillar of hair. "It won't work on me."

I deflate.

"But it wasn't us," says Vi. "It really wasn't."

Dr. Thalassi looks at us one at a time. Then he nods. He lifts the umbrella off the desk and drops it into a brass stand nearby.

"I know it wasn't," he says after a moment. "The glass is all on the outside. Whoever broke that window was inside the museum already."

"Ow, it's starting to hurt," says Violet, clutching her cheek. The doctor has already given her a wad of cotton, soaked in disinfectant, to hold against it. The cotton wad is pink with blood.

"Let me see," says the doctor. He gets to his feet and allows his specs to drop down onto his nose as he peers at the wound.

"This wasn't done by glass," he says. "It looks for all the world like something scratched you. Something big."

Violet and I exchange glances again, but there doesn't seem to be any point to beating around this particular supernatural bush.

"Dr. Thalassi," says Vi, "do you believe in the malamander?"

The doctor sits back, making his chair creak, and places his fingertips together in a steeple. Since he's also wearing a swirly dressing gown, he reminds me for a moment of Sherlock Holmes.

"Interesting question," he says. "A legendary aquatic creature, entirely unknown to science, that is rumored to haunt these shores and which is occasionally sighted by the townsfolk as they roll home from the pub at midnight. And for which there isn't a shred of evidence, I might add. Do *you* think this is something I should believe in?"

"When you say it like that, it sounds silly," says Violet. "But what about Mrs. Fossil's arm? You said yourself she'd been bitten. The curve of that bite was right across her forearm and hand. Surely that was done by something big, too. Isn't that evidence?"

"Hmm." The doctor narrows his eyes. "Let's say for a moment

that I do believe. Or let's say, at least, that I believe it is possible, which is not quite the same thing. Why would such a creature be inside my museum, behind locked doors, at night?"

"It might," says Violet, meeting his gaze, "if it were looking for something."

The doctor's eyebrow slowly creeps up again.

Violet pulls out her book and lays it on the desk in front of her. From where I sit, I can see MALAMANDER written across the sea-green cover in faded bronze letters.

"When I was given this book by the mermonkey, I thought it was just a story. Just a local legend. But since then, I've seen things — twice now — that I can't explain. And I've found things out, too. Like the fact that my dad believed the creature described in this book is real. And if it *is* real, then what about other things in the book?"

"What other things?" says the doc.

"I think you know."

Dr. Thalassi stares at Violet. Then he puts one hand into his dressing gown pocket and pulls something out. He places it gently on the desk between us. It's roughly the size and shape of a very large egg, ruby red in color and glowing faintly in the light of the lamp.

"The malamander egg," says Violet in a whisper.

"Or," says the doctor, "a piece of harmless red sea glass, found by Mrs. Fossil, which just happens to be egg-shaped. Which is a great deal more likely, wouldn't you agree?"

"But if it's just that," I say, "why do you want it?"

The doc smiles. He picks up the paraffin lamp and moves it across his desk. The egg-shaped glass lump, or whatever it is, glows brighter and fiercer as the lamp approaches, then fainter again as it moves away.

Like a winking red star.

"You were trying to lure it here!" Violet cries. "Up in your tower, shining that red light. You were trying to lure the malamander!"

"If," says the doc, raising a finger, "and it's still a big 'if,' the malamander is real, then it bit Mrs. Fossil for a reason. Maybe it mistook this piece of red glass for something else, if only for a moment. That is a hypothesis that can only be tested by experiment . . ."

"But it's a monster!"

"By *experiment*," the doc insists, "to gather evidence . . ."

"An experiment that just slashed off half of Vi's face!" I blurt out. "Is that evidence enough for you?"

OK, the half-a-face thing is a teensy bit of an exaggeration, but the doc sighs and has the decency to look sheepish anyway. His eyebrows seem to flock from one side of his forehead to the other.

"Don't forget that you're the intruders here, Herbie," he says eventually, slipping the lump of sea glass back into his pocket. "It was not my intention to cause anyone any harm."

Awkward silence.

Then the doc changes the subject by reaching out and picking up Violet's book.

"*Malamander*, by Captain K," he says. "One of the more interesting tales associated with the legend. Jenny told me you were dispensed this. I have a copy myself, of course, but mine doesn't have seaweed stains on it. Have you finished reading it yet?"

Violet says nothing, so I pipe up.

"I haven't read *any* of it, Doc. Though, I'm beginning to think I should."

"Everyone who lives in Eerie-on-Sea should read this book, Herbie," says Dr. Thalassi, waggling it at me.

"I'll add it to my to-do list. In the meantime, could you give me the nutshell version, please, Doc? I don't mind spoilers."

Dr. Thalassi leans back in his chair again. The paraffin lamp hisses softly on his desk, making the shadows dance in the room.

"Very well," he says.

CHAPTER 21

LEVIATHAN

Captain K was commander of the warship *Leviathan* during the later years of Queen Victoria's reign," says Dr. Thalassi. "He was patrolling the far north when he discovered a floating island of rock and ice that wasn't on any chart. Through his telescope, he spied a vast glittering cavern in the island. Under the glow of the aurora borealis, Captain K ordered a boat to be lowered into the sea and had himself rowed over through the wind and snow to explore.

"As the boat entered the cavern, there came a terrible sound—a screeching, wailing roar that filled the seamen with dread. They wanted to turn back.

"'Since when have sailors been scared of the wind?' said Captain K, and he ordered them to row on.

"The cavern led to the heart of the island. There they found a great stinking mound of seaweed, bones, and shipwreck salvage. At the top of the mound was an eerie red glow. The men again asked to turn back, but again the captain called them cowards. He stepped out onto the seaweed mound himself and began to climb."

"Brave," I say. "But I think he should have listened to his men."

Dr. Thalassi shrugs.

"Maybe so. Anyway, when he reached the top of the mound, he found that the mound was actually a gigantic nest. For resting in a little dip on the summit, Captain K found a large red crystal egg, glowing with its own internal light."

"How can it be an egg if it's made of crystal?" I say.

"Do you want me to tell the story," says the doc, "or answer all your questions?"

I zip my mouth shut with an okeydoke grin.

"Captain K had never seen anything like this strange egg, yet it seemed oddly familiar, like something from a story, half forgotten. He picked up the egg and gasped at the warmth of it. It seemed to vibrate with creative promise, as if all it were waiting for was something to realize its magical potential. Or someone.

In the captain's wondering mind, a thousand voices seemed to whisper as one: *I can make your dreams come true.*

"Captain K shook his head. He didn't have time for magical voices and fairy-tale nonsense. On the other hand, a glowing red crystal the size of an ostrich egg? Why, that would certainly make a fine trophy for his mantelpiece back home. So he tucked the pretty thing in the crook of his arm. He hardly heard the terrible shrieking roar that sounded again as he slid back down to the boat and ordered his men to row for the ship.

"It was only later, as dawn broke and *Leviathan* was steaming southward, away from the strange floating island, that the captain remembered the legend of the malamander. He had grown up in the town of Eerie, you see, and had spent many a sleepless childhood night trying not to think about the terrible monster in the old tales.

"'Didn't that lay a glowing red egg, too?' he muttered to himself. 'In the stories? And wasn't there something about the egg having the power to grant wishes?'

"But as I've already said, Captain K didn't believe in magic and nonsense. Nevertheless, he ordered the ship's speed to be increased, just in case.

"It was that night that the monster attacked.

"The men weren't prepared. Many lives were lost defending *Leviathan* against the creature, which bristled with fins and quivering spines and terrified all who saw it. Bullets sparked off its scales, leaving scarcely a mark, and its claws could rend iron. By dawn the men had driven it off, but the sun rose over a ship in a terrible state.

"The next night, the men were better prepared and armed to the teeth. They fought bravely and in good formation, and again the creature was driven off, but again the cost was cripplingly high. As the sun rose on the aftermath, the mighty battleship was listing in the water, and the loss of men was appalling.

"'It comes for its egg!' the surviving sailors cried to the captain. 'For the love of grog, give it back its egg!'

"Captain K, alone in his cabin, had come to the same conclusion. He brought the egg out of its hiding place and wondered if he should throw it in the sea. After all, good men were dying so that he could keep it. But the egg dazzled him with its beauty and thrilled him with its strange promise. There was no way he could give up such a wondrous thing.

"'So what if the malamander is real after all?' said the captain to himself, gazing into the magical light of the creature's egg. 'It's still just a dumb animal, while I'm a man, and commander of one of the most powerful vessels in the fleet.'

"The thousandfold voice whispered in his mind again: *I can make your dreams come true. I can grant your heart's desire.*

"'My wish right now is to survive this,' said the captain,

almost without thinking. 'I don't want to be killed like a rat in a barrel by this fiendish creature.' Then he added, because he suddenly realized it was his heart's desire, 'I want to live forever.'

"Then you shall, said the voice. *For as long as you can keep the egg. But if you lose it, your wish shall become your curse.*

" 'Fight harder!' the captain roared to his men. 'Prepare yourselves! Defend the ship at all costs!'

"The third night brought the strongest attack yet. The captain and the remains of his crew barricaded themselves on the bridge and fought to hold the malamander back. The captain himself received many injuries, but a strange thing happened: a sea mist, which came out of nowhere, surrounded Captain K, and his wounds closed up as soon as they opened, and his injuries healed. The exhaustion of battle left him, and he knew that the egg, tucked safely in the pocket of his greatcoat, was indeed granting him his wish. He knew that he would survive the fight, that he would live forever.

"But that's more than could be said for his crew. By the time the dawn came and the monster had once again withdrawn, barely a handful remained. The *Leviathan,* which was billowing smoke and listing even farther in the water, was directed at war speed toward Eerie-on-Sea, its engines hot and rumbling as the men burned everything in sight to create steam. The malamander was an Eerie legend, the captain reasoned, and maybe—just maybe—if they could lead it home, the monster would leave them alone."

Dr. Thalassi pauses and looks thoughtfully into the paraffin lamp.

"And?" says Violet after a moment, pulling her coat closer. "Don't stop now. Did it leave them alone?"

The doctor lowers his brow.

"They approached the town the following day, at dusk, steaming at a reckless rate. Far from leaving them alone, the monster attacked the moment the sun went down. With the last of his men stationed in the engine room—ordered to keep course for Eerie-on-Sea—Captain K went out onto the deck to face the malamander alone."

"That's bonkers!" I say.

"Indeed," says the doc. "Very bonkers. But the captain was drunk with power. He had the magical egg, after all, and he knew he would live forever as long as he possessed it. He felt invincible. And according to legend, the malamander, though tough as steel, was *not* invincible. It had one weakness. It *could* be killed. At least, that's what the stories said. Captain K thought that with the magic on his side, he would find that weakness and finish the beast off for good."

"Only, that's not what happened," says Violet.

Dr. Thalassi shakes his head.

"Whether it was some treachery in the magic, or some miscalculation on the part of the captain, this was to be his last stand. As he faced up to the monster on the heaving deck, wreathed in the strange sea mist, clutching the egg like a weapon, the creature darted forward and delivered a bite. A good, hard bite, which injected stinging venom. The bite hurt, but the real terror wasn't in the pain. It was in the cold numbness that froze the captain's limbs. He lost the ability to move down one side of his body and he fell. In horror, Captain K could only watch as the malamander bent over him and with a single snap of its jaws tore his right hand—the hand that held the malamander egg—clean off and swallowed it whole."

"So he lost it," I say, after a pause to let the gory details sink in. "The egg. But doesn't that mean the wish would become a curse?"

"I'm glad you were paying attention, Herbie," says the doc with a nod. "The malamander, having devoured its magical egg once again, slipped into the sea with a final roar and was gone. The ship ran aground, of course, and the last of the crew abandoned the wreck. As for the captain, with the magic gone, all the wounds he had received during the battle returned. He was found on the deck by some brave souls from Eerie, a ruin of a man, ranting and raving, and waving the stump where his hand used to be, vowing revenge against the malamander.

"In the days that followed, he had something grafted on his arm in place of the lost hand, something he could use as a weapon. And they say he spent the rest of his days hunting for the monster that had destroyed him."

I look at Vi, and she looks at me.

"The something," I say, with a slightly wobbly voice, "the something he had grafted on instead of a hand. I, er, I don't suppose the book says anything about what that something might have been?"

"It does, as it happens," says Dr. Thalassi. "It was a boat hook."

CHAPTER 22

THE EERIE MUSEUM

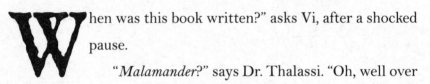

"When was this book written?" asks Vi, after a shocked pause.

"*Malamander*?" says Dr. Thalassi. "Oh, well over a century ago. I'd have to look it up."

Violet turns to me. "It must be a coincidence, surely."

"A coincidence?" asks the doctor. "What is a coincidence?"

"What happened to Captain K?" Violet ignores the question by asking one of her own. "In the end?"

"No one knows for sure," says the doctor. "Some say that even now he can sometimes be seen, wandering at night near the wreck, searching for the monster and his revenge. But that can't be true. He must be long dead."

"Are there any pictures of Captain K?" I ask, almost without squeaking. "Any old photos?"

"This is a museum," says Dr. Thalassi. "Of course there are old photos."

⚙○✿

We're in the main exhibition space of the Eerie Museum, in the softly fizzing glow of the paraffin lantern. Above us the skeleton of a whale hangs suspended, and in the cabinets all around, stuffed and desiccated sea creatures peer out at us through glass eyes.

"Over here," says the doctor, leading us to the far wall. "This display concerns the wrecking of the *Leviathan*."

And there, among the nautical charts and brass instruments of navigation, we see what, by now, we are both dreading: a faded sepia photo of a man in a captain's uniform, standing on the deck of an immense iron warship. This man is less grotesque, and with a neater, trimmer beard, but there's no mistaking him.

"Boat Hook Man," Violet whispers.

"He doesn't have a boat hook for a hand in this picture," I say.

"He wouldn't." The doctor holds the lamp even closer, so we can read the caption. "This was taken five years before all that happened. He was sixty years old at the time."

"But that would make him . . ." I say, working it out roughly in my head, "going on two hundred years old! He can't be."

Violet looks as shocked as I feel. Dr. Thalassi watches us
with an inscrutable expression.

"It almost sounds," he says, after a moment, "as if you think you've met Captain K. Even though that would be completely impossible."

"Yeah," I say, "completely impossible."

"Why is it so cold in here?" Violet pulls her coat tightly around herself.

"A window was broken, remember?" says the doctor. "I had better cover it up for the rest of the night, or I could have more intruders. You two can help me. Then I'll walk you home."

"How did it get in?" I say. "The, er, 'intruder,' I mean. All the other windows seem intact."

"They are," says the doctor, "but can you smell something unusual, Herbie Lemon? Something that will give you a clue?"

I sniff. The place smells of beeswax polish and ancient wood and preserving fluid and old, old stone. And something else.

"Soot?" says Vi, also sniffing.

Together we turn to a huge medieval fireplace—deep enough to stand in—that reaches up one of the walls.

"It doesn't look as if a fire has been lit in here for years," says Violet as we step inside and look up. Far above, a rectangle of cold night sky is visible, a single shimmering star winking in the center.

"Not for centuries," agrees Dr. Thalassi. "And yet, look down."

We do so. There are newly fallen flakes of blackened stone and brick on the hearthstones, which crunch underfoot.

"It came down the chimney," I say, looking back up again.

"Someone did, at least," says the doc.

"Wait! What's that?" asks Vi, pointing up. The doctor lifts the lantern and something gleams, stuck between two stones. The doctor reaches up and plucks it out. He holds it to the lantern, and we gather around the object in his fingertips.

It's a scale — rigid and sharp and iridescent with purples and greens.

And big.

"Evidence?" says Violet, glancing at the doctor.

"Hmm," says the doctor, slipping the scale into his waistcoat pocket.

⚙

Fixing a piece of board over the broken window takes less time than I expected. With the doctor up the ladder, and me passing nails, Violet has nothing to do but hold the doc's dressing gown while she waits for us to finish.

Dr. Thalassi insists on walking us back to the hotel. But I'm a bit nervous — I'm still keeping Violet a secret, remember? — and I manage to persuade him to leave us at the corner of Spindrift Alley, a little way from the hotel entrance. We watch as he strolls back up to his museum, swinging his umbrella. He lifts his astra-khan hat to say goodbye, and then he's gone.

Back in the hotel, I'm disappointed to see that Amber Griss is still on duty at Reception, which means that she at least knows how late I got back. She gives me a wink, which means she prob-ably won't tell old Mollusc, but I can't be sure. There is a pile of stuff for me to sort through on my cubbyhole desk. I grab it and vanish down to my cellar, where, of course, the wood burner is now midnight cold. I open the window and Violet hops down.

"We need to decide what we're going to do next," she says, but I hold up my hand.

"Oh, no, we need to sleep." I chuck my cap into the corner and flop down in my chair. "I've had more than enough of today, thanks. Let's see how it all looks tomorrow."

"OK, then," says Violet, more meekly than I was expecting. "Sleep well, Herbie. And maybe barricade the window, just in case."

"Why on earth should I do that?" I reply, frowning, because that's a funny thing to say.

"Well, if what we learned today about the malamander and its egg is true"—Violet smiles strangely, heading toward her bed of coats—"we might get a visitor in the night."

"Wait," I say, sitting up. "What have you done?"

"Me?"

"Yes, you! Why do you look so pleased with yourself?"

"I'm just saying that we should be careful, that's all," she says, and that's when I notice that she's fiddling with something in her coat pocket. An image of Violet holding the doc's dressing gown while we fixed the window flashes into my head, and I gasp.

"You didn't!"

"I did." Violet grins, and she pulls out her hand. The egg-shaped stone that Mrs. Fossil found on the beach, and which the doctor placed on his desk as he told us the fantastic, tragic story of Captain K, gleams brilliant ruby red in her palm.

CHAPTER 23

MR. MOLLUSC

It's f-till f-tealing," I say to Violet the next morning as I struggle to get my teeth through my very stale breakfast. "What-effer else you want to call it."

"Is it really stealing, though?" says Vi, turning the egg-shaped stone in her hand. "Two days ago it was just lying on the beach with no owner at all."

"A lot has happened in those two days, Vi."

"I know, but, Herbie . . ." Violet says, holding her prize up to the light. "What if this is a real malamander egg?"

"It's too small," I say with a snort. "Besides, the malamander chased Captain K across the Atlantic to get its egg back and wrecked a battleship doing it. Do you really think it would just leave its egg lying around on a beach? Or allow Dr. Thalassi to wander around with it in his dressing gown pocket?"

"No, but—"

"Vi," I say, giving her one of my most discouraging looks, "what you have there is just a lump of sea glass. A *stolen* lump, at that. I'm not really sure why you took it."

Vi glares back at me, then slips the red stone back into her pocket.

"Because," she says, "whether it's real or not, Dr. Thalassi was using it last night to attract the malamander. And I don't think that's something anyone should be doing, do you?"

"Maybe not, but I'm expecting the doc to come hammering on my cubbyhole any moment now. Demanding it back."

"Then we'll just say that we found it." Violet gives me a beaming smile. "And you can return it to him, Herbie. That's your job, after all."

Through the cellar window I see that it's snowing — properly snowing this time, with great fat flakes that fall like marshmallows. I've got my burner fired up, and it's nice not to have to go out into that cold just yet, but to sit instead in the warm glow and chat with Violet about mysteries and magic. And, for the first time in a long time, not feel quite so alone.

"Anyway, I haven't exactly had any of my wishes come true," says Violet, looking sadly at her rock-hard croissant. "Have you?"

I glance at her again but decide to say nothing.

Once breakfast is finished, I straighten my uniform and pop my Lost-and-Founder's cap on, managing not to ping the elastic this time.

"I need to work, Vi. Lost things were handed in yesterday, and I've got to look busy in front of old Mollusc, or I'll be on the chopping block. You should stay down here, where it's safe, and give the whole strange business a good thinking over. I'll be back around lunchtime and we can talk then."

But when I get up to my cubbyhole, I find that old Mollusc is already there. He leers in over my desk, twitching his horrible mustache.

"To whom were you talking, Lemon?"

I say the bad word again—only, inside my head this time.

"Just to myself, sir," I say. "Sometimes it's the only way I can get an intelligent conversation around here."

The hotel manager glares at me, his mouth pursed like a cat's bum. Then he jerks open a tape measure and lays it across the opening to my Lost-and-Foundery.

"Pah! Too small," he mutters. "I had plans to fit a toothbrush dispenser in here, but it looks as though I'll just get it boarded up, after all. With you and the rest of the rubbish still inside."

"Have you lost something, sir?" I say. "Your marbles, perhaps?"

"I am about to lose something, yes." Mr. Mollusc grins and snaps the tape measure shut. "For good. You're out, Herbert Lemon. Fired!"

And with that he drops a letter onto the desk in front of me and stalks off, chuckling to himself.

I look at the letter. He can't fire me; only Lady Kraken can do that. And as Lady Kraken says herself, there has always been a Lost-and-Founder at the Grand Nautilus Hotel. But I can see Lady K's spider writing on the envelope. I go to tear it open and find it's been peeled open already.

Mr. Mollusc has read it.

I pull the note out and read it myself.

Herbert Lemon,

I know what you did last night. I am extremely disappointed in you. Come to my room immediately.

Lady Kraken

⚙○✿

I reach the door to the Jules Verne Suite. Along the corridor behind me, I can feel the painted eyes of the Kraken family glaring down from their picture frames.

How could I have been so stupid? How could I have forgotten the cameraluna?

I reach out and pull the cord and hear the distant *ding* of the bell. The COME IN light flashes on immediately, and the door swings open.

Lady Kraken's enormous curtain-shrouded sitting room is lit with cold light from an open French window. In the window, her back to me, Lady Kraken herself sits in her bronze-and-wicker wheelchair, wrapped in a shawl. Beyond is a balcony, white with the snow that falls and swirls around the old lady.

I step forward into the icy-cold room and try a cough — a small "Here I am" one.

After a moment, Lady Kraken lifts one claw hand and beckons me over. The door behind me swings shut with a coffin-lid thud.

"See how clean the town looks?" says Lady Kraken as I reach her side. "The snow covers all the grime, all the strangeness of the place. It makes everything seem new again."

I make a small, polite noise. It's a step up from the cough, but not a big one.

"But it wasn't snowing last night, was it, Mr. Lemon? Last night there was a beautiful full moon. I could see" — and she turns her wheelchair sharply — "everything!"

"I can explain!" I blurt out.

The claw hand is raised again as the lady points to my face.

"You saw it, didn't you?"

"Yes!"

"Face-to-face! Saw the full horror of it." Her eyes are flashing. "Saw with your own eyes the monstrosity that haunts our town."

I step back, clutching my cap to my chest.

"Lady Kraken, Your Grandness, I was going to tell you, I promise . . ."

"You did promise, didn't you, Mr. Lemon?" Lady Kraken's chair whirs into electric life as she advances toward me. "Promised to be my eyes and ears. So, tell me now! Why was the creature at the museum? Why were *you* there?"

"I—I don't know," I manage to say, backing into a table. It's the very table Lady K uses to display the images with her cameraluna. "That is to say, I *do* know. I just don't really know what it all means. . . ."

Lady Kraken creaks to a halt right in front of me.

"Are you always such a dunderbrain, boy?" she croaks. "Surely this means that Dr. Thalassi is up to something."

I manage a shrug.

"And how about that other one?" says Lady Kraken. "The girl. Oh, yes, Herbert Lemon, I know all about the girl. Something else you were going to tell me, I suppose?"

I grin; though, the grin must look a bit desperate. The cap in my hand is crushed now, my knuckles white.

"So, why haven't you reported back?" Lady Kraken says. "Something is stirring in this town, plots are thickening, threads are coming together, and I am just a frail old lady with a camera-luna. I need you to help me, Herbert Lemon. I need you to help me before it's too late and someone else gets the egg!"

"What!" I say, blinking. "You want the egg, too?"

I wasn't expecting this.

"I bet they are in it together," says Lady K, ignoring my question. "Dr. Thalassi and the girl. Working hand in glove, no doubt. A great conspiracy of scheming and plot to take what's rightfully mine."

"The egg is rightfully yours?" I say. I'm still blinking.

"Have you cloth for brains, boy?" Lady Kraken croaks. "Haven't you figured it out yet? Of course it's rightfully mine. It destroyed my grandfather, then it destroyed my whole family as we fought to end the curse and put things right. It has taken everyone I loved: dear Father, my brothers, my sister even, when she, too, tried her hand at claiming the monster's egg."

She pauses for a gasp of breath. Then continues.

"But if Grandfather has returned, then there is hope again. Maybe finally we can regain the malamander egg and I can use its power to wish my family back to life! That egg is rightfully mine. No one has paid a higher price for it than I. And with its power, I could end my grandfather's curse and set the Kraken family free."

"Your grandfather?" I say, light slowly dawning in my poor rattled brain box. "You mean . . . ?"

I gulp.

"You mean Boat Hook Man is your *grandfather*?"

"*Captain Kraken* is my grandfather." The old lady narrows her eyes at me. "This, this *Boat Hook Man*, as you call him, is merely the wisp that remains on earth, growing thinner every year, destined to never die because he lost the egg. But with the power of the malamander egg, I could make him a real man once again. He can be set free!"

"But," I can't help saying aloud, looking at the wizened old woman in her antique electric wheelchair, "how are you going to get the egg?"

Lady Kraken grins her turtle grin.

"I'm not, Mr. Lemon. *You* are going to get it for me."

CHAPTER 24

A KRAKEN'S-EYE VIEW

F irst," says Lady Kraken as I sit down heavily in an armchair, "you are going to tell me exactly what Dr. Thalassi and the girl are up to."

With a swipe of her hand, the old lady flips a switch on her control box. The French windows swing closed behind her in a last flurry of snow.

"But, Your Ladyness, you've got it wrong," I say. "The doc and Violet aren't working together at all."

"Violet?" asks Lady Kraken.

"Yes, the girl. She's Violet Parma. She's not after any magical egg. She just wants her mum and dad back."

"Parma?" Lady Kraken taps the arm of her chair. "That name . . . where have I heard it before?"

"Her father was—sorry—*is* Peter Parma," I say. "Only, he's missing, and —"

"Now I remember," Lady Kraken says, cracking all her knuckles at once. "The folklorist, the collector of old tales. He spent many hours here, interviewing me about my family. I liked him well enough at the beginning, but in the end he asked too many questions, pried too deep into my family's misfortune. I have no doubt he wanted the egg, too, and no doubt that the malamander devoured him for his trouble."

"Oh!" I say. "No doubt at all?"

"None whatsoever," snaps the old lady. "But it gives this Violet a good motive to get hold of the egg for herself, doesn't it? She could wish him back to life."

"But . . ." I try to say.

"So, what of Dr. Thalassi?" Lady Kraken plows on. "He's always been a sly one, that doctor. What part does he play in all this?"

"I think he's just after evidence," I say, thinking back to our conversation in the museum. "I think he just wants to prove one way or another if the creature exists. He's a scientist."

"Ha! A likely excuse."

I sit up and put my Lost-and-Founder's cap firmly back on my head.

"Lady Kraken, I promise you, you have it all wrong. I mean, yes, you're right, someone is after the egg. But it's not the doc, and it's not Vi. I think it's Sebastian Eels."

Now it's Lady Kraken's turn to blink with surprise.

"The writer?"

"He's certainly acting very suspiciously," I say.

"But, then, Mr. Lemon, I am mistaken after all," says Lady K, scratching her chin as she tumbles this new idea around in her mind. "You are right. The girl isn't working with Dr. Thalassi. . . ."

"Exactly," I say.

"She's working with Sebastian Eels instead."

"What?"

"Suddenly it all makes sense." Lady Kraken brings her fist down on the arm of her chair with a bony thud. "How could I have been so blind? How could I have missed it? And how could you, Mr. Lemon, have been such an incorrigible dunderbrain as to allow this to happen?"

"Me?" I say, shrinking back again.

"Yes, you. Can't you see how you've been used? Can't you see how this girl has tricked you? You've been duped, Herbert Lemon. Violet Parma is playing you for a fool."

"B . . ." I almost manage to say.

"Oh, don't try to argue," says Lady K. "It all falls into place;

the connections become clear. I know Eels and the Parma girl are in this together. I have proof."

With a flick of several switches on the old lady's wheelchair, the curtains in the room swish shut, one after another. The lights go out, and there's a whirring sound in the ceiling. I look up to see a hole opening in the ornate plaster high above us. Then a shaft of ghostly light flickers on, shining directly down onto the circular table in the center of the room, as the cameraluna hums into life.

"I recorded this three nights ago," says Lady Kraken as the moon-bright dust motes begin to dance on the tabletop. "Just after dusk."

"It can *record* as well?" I say, but Lady Kraken just waves my surprise away.

"Of course it can record. It's a cameraluna."

As I watch, the dust and light form into an eerie, shimmering model of the town again, in three dimensions. But just as I get my bearings, Lady Kraken begins turning dials, and the image swirls and changes. Little figures of the townsfolk dart around, walking backward at high speed, as if we are going back in time, and the light comes and goes with the passing of the clouds. Then the image stabilizes at last, as the lady zeroes in on a particular moment, and a particular place.

"That's Sebastian Eels's house!" I say.

Sure enough, the author's tall, stately town house—one of the finest in Eerie-on-Sea—rises up on the table before me in shimmering, dusty detail. As I watch, amazed, I see a tiny figure of Eels himself emerge from the front door of this model house, straighten his neatly folded scarf, and stride off along the tiny street.

"Now, watch closely," says Lady Kraken, dimly lit in the captured moonlight of the past. "Just about . . . *now!*"

And she points her crooked finger.

An even smaller figure appears at the end of the miniature street. It darts into a doorway before reemerging and creeping ahead, heading always for Eels's house. I stare in amazement—there's no mistaking the catlike way the figure moves, or the mass of crazy curls on her head. Or the woolly bobble hat.

It's Violet.

"This can't be *dusk* three nights ago," I say, though even as I say it, I cannot help believing that it is. Lady Kraken may have some bonkers ideas, but if there's one thing she's an expert on, it's cameralunas. But since Violet didn't appear at the hotel till long after nightfall, this recording must have been made hours earlier. In other words, hours before I first met her.

"Keep watching," says Lady Kraken.

So I do. And I see the little figure of Violet stop outside the house. She goes up to the door and rings the bell. Then she rings it again. No one answers. I watch in shocked fascination as the tiny silvery figure of Violet Parma walks over to a low wall beside the house and lifts herself into the branch of an overhanging tree. She runs up it and drops down the other side of the wall into darkness — an empty patch that the cameraluna can't reach. A moment or two later, she appears again, climbing into the house of Sebastian Eels by an open window and, again, vanishing from view.

Then, as suddenly as it all began, the light of the cameraluna shuts off and the fairy model of the house collapses into dust. We are plunged into darkness once again. With a flick of a switch, Lady K opens the curtains.

"So, Mr. Lemon," she says. "Still sure about that sneaky little friend of yours? In fact, how can you be certain she's even looking for her parents at all? How do you know they aren't here, too, hiding, plotting with Sebastian Eels? Yes, I'll wager they are all in it together, conspiring against me, conspiring to get my malamander egg!"

I stagger to my feet and stumble back toward the door.

"But . . . but . . ."

"*Still* don't believe me, Mr. Lemon?" Lady Kraken continues, her eyes wild. "Then just ask yourself one question: What is Violet Parma doing when you aren't with her?"

"But . . ."

"Just ask yourself, what is Violet Parma doing *right now?*"

I hear the door swing open behind me. I back out through it in a haze of doubt.

By the time the door is closed again, I'm running.

I run back along the corridor and down the stairs, three at a time. In Reception I don't even slow as I dodge around some guests and their cases and hear Amber Griss tut-tutting me. I throw open the desk of my cubbyhole and clatter down to my cellar.

"Violet!" I call. "Vi!"

But there's no answer.

She isn't there.

CHAPTER 25

MYSTERIOUS VISITORS

I close my eyes and take a moment to calm myself.

"It can't be true," I say under my breath. "Can it?"

Then I open my eyes and see that Violet's coat is gone, as well as her mother's boots. Violet has definitely gone out somewhere.

I shake my head and try to forget Lady K's accusation.

After all, so what? Why *shouldn't* she go out somewhere? She's free to come and go, isn't she? I'm not her keeper. But then again, where would she go? She's still new to the town. Or so she says.

There's no escaping the fact that I said I'd be out till lunchtime, and here I am, hours earlier than expected, and she's not here.

And what about the cameraluna? What about the moon-light recording I saw? Violet went to see Eels *before* she came to see me.

Suddenly I remember how Violet never did explain why Boat Hook Man was chasing her. Was that whole episode just an elaborate way to gain my trust? Was that whole episode *staged*?

I grab my Lost-and-Founder's cap with both hands, pull it up as high as I can on the elastic, and let it snap down onto my head. It stings, but it clears my head a little and helps me switch on my logic.

"There's an innocent explanation," I say aloud. "There has to be. And I need to find it."

I look at the window. It's slightly open, so Violet probably left that way. At least that means she wasn't caught by old Mollusc. But where has she gone?

I screw my hands into my eyes as I try to think it through.

She probably hasn't gone to see Jenny Hanniver at the Eerie Book Dispensary, because we already spoke with Jenny yester-day. And probably she wouldn't dare go back to the museum. Unless, she wanted to return the sea glass? But somehow, I don't think she's ready to do that. So . . . where?

The beach? On her own? That's possible.

But there's another very disturbing possibility.

I grab my coat.

I slip two hot pebbles into my pockets, put the CLOSED sign up on my cubbyhole, and run out into the snowy town.

Sebastian Eels's tall town house looked grand enough built of motes and moonlight on Lady Kraken's table, but it is grander still in real life. It's perched high in the town, its top floor windows giving a commanding view of the bay, surpassed only by that of the Grand Nautilus Hotel below on the seafront. It is painted yellow and has an imposing black door with white columns on either side. Today, in the snow, it is silent, its eight large front windows empty and dark.

I check the street outside and see several tracks in the snow, including one large set of footprints that emerge from the door of the house. At a guess, I would say that these were made by Eels himself. The footprints show someone leaving but no one coming back.

At the side of the house is a wall, peeling yellow, with a garden beyond. I recognize it from the image in the cameraluna. The branch of a gnarled old tree leans over into the street. And there are smaller footprints leading to it but not leading away.

I look up at the house to see if any windows are open. And that's when I notice him.

Erwin.

The cat is sitting on top of a nearby wall, watching me with his cool blue eyes.

"Did she come this way, then?" I ask.

"P-RRRR," says Erwin, licking one paw.

"Fat lot of help you are," I say, grabbing the branch anyway. I swing toward the wall. A moment of scrabbling later, and then I'm over the top, tumbling down into a prickly bush on the other side.

"Argh! Bladderwracks!" I cry out as quietly as I can.

I get up and pick thorns out of my coat, and I see that a ground floor window is slightly open, just as it must have been three nights ago.

"You could have warned me about the bush," I whisper up to Erwin, but he's no longer there.

Through the window I see some kind of pantry or larder. It's hard to see much, but on the tiles just inside the window I spot a patch of melting snow, and somehow I just know that Violet left it there.

I heave myself up onto the sill and slide through the open window.

There's a table in front of me, and I have to bite my tongue to stop myself from crying out when I see what's lying there. A human body! Except, not exactly. At a second glance I realize it is actually something human body *shaped*.

"A wet suit?" I say aloud.

And it is. But not the kind you might use for snorkeling on vacation — this is a serious set, complete with air tanks, a helmet, and head lamps. There are other things there too. Strange things: lengths of old rubber hose, a saw with long jagged teeth, pneumatic harpoon guns.

There is also a pile of cardboard targets, like the ones you get at shooting galleries. I can't help noticing that on each target, the bull's-eye is riddled with holes. Whoever fired at them is a crack shot.

And is this armor? I gasp at the sight of a steel chain-mail shirt on a hanger. I touch it and feel its shiny metal links slip between my fingers, like scales.

A faint noise somewhere in the house jolts me. I mustn't waste time. Sebastian Eels could be home at any moment. I slide the window almost all the way down, so that it looks closed at a glance but can still be opened in a hurry, and continue into the house.

In the wide entrance hall there are small drops of melted snow at the bottom of a broad wooden staircase. My heart is pounding as I set off up the steps, trying not to make them creak.

On the second floor is a long landing with a number of doors. One is slightly ajar, and there are rustling sounds from inside. I edge toward it.

"Violet!" I whisper-shout. "Violet, is that you?"

But what if it isn't?

What if all I'm doing is letting someone else—Eels himself, perhaps, or Boat Hook Man—know that I'm there?

This is ridiculous—I shouldn't be here. Yet, since I *am* here, I have to check. I brace myself to run if I need to, but I take another step toward the door.

There's a loud *click* and a *clunk* from downstairs. It's the sound of the front door being unlocked and opened, followed by the noise of large booted feet stamping off snow.

"Come in, my old friends" comes a voice I know too well, and I hear two other sets of feet enter the house. "It's a long time since I welcomed you here."

Sebastian Eels is home!

CHAPTER 26

A STUDY IN VIOLET

I push my way into the room where I heard the rustling, and I swing the door silently behind me, leaving it open just a sliver.

"Herbie!" Violet looks up from a pile of papers on a desk, astonishment on her face. "Herbie, what are you doing here?"

I give her a look. I could ask her the same question!

The book-lined room is clearly a study, with a large desk filling the window. Carved in the middle of it is an old map of the town and harbor, with arrows and markings drawn all over it. Beside the desk is a plan chest with several of its drawers open, and nearby are boxes of paper notes and charts, many of them scattered over the floor, along with an empty bottle of whiskey.

"Did you make all this mess?" I whisper.

"No! Do you think I drink whiskey?"

I silence her with my hand and listen through the door. There is the hum of conversation downstairs, but I can't make out the voices now. It sounds as though Eels and his visitors have gone into another room.

"How did you know I'd be here?" Violet demands.

"No, Violet," I say, "I think the question we should really be asking is, how do you know where Sebastian Eels lives?"

"What . . . ?" says Violet, looking suddenly flustered. "What do you mean?"

"I mean," I say, letting my eyes narrow, "I don't remember telling you where he lives. And yet here you are, looking pretty cozy up in his study."

Violet opens her mouth, then closes it again.

"No clever answer?" I say, my mind full of the things Lady K said to me, which suddenly don't seem so crazy. "That's not like you. Is there something you're not telling me, Violet?"

"No, of course not."

Violet looks confused. Or is that more of a guilty expression?

"So," I say, "how *did* you know Sebastian Eels's address?"

"I—I just found out, that's all."

"Really?" I give her my archest eyebrow.

"It doesn't matter." Violet waves the eyebrow away. "What

matters right now is how we are going to get away now that Eels has come back."

And she tiptoes to the door and slips out, completely side-stepping my question. Something, I realize, she's very good at.

I follow her through the door and onto the landing. The voices are still rumbling somewhere below, just out of earshot.

"We could run down," Violet whispers, "and try to get out the pantry window before they hear us."

I shake my head.

"And what if they're *in* the pantry?"

"Well, what, then?" asks Violet.

Suddenly the voices get much louder as Eels and his guests come back toward the hall. With the way down blocked, Violet and I get ready to rush farther up the stairs, if need be, to the floor above.

But first we strain to listen.

"Tonight, of course," says the voice of Eels. "It's Midwinter, after all. The longest night of the year, and an exceptionally low tide."

Then a woman says something in reply, but I don't catch it.

"Who could it be?" Violet whispers in my ear. "Sounds like a man and woman."

I look at her.

"You really don't know?" I say.

"Herbie, what is this? What's gotten into you? Of course I don't know."

"There is no need to worry" comes the booming voice of Eels again, and we hear the front door opening. "I merely wish to observe the animal, that's all. The weapon will be for protection only, to scare it away if I'm seen. Goodbye."

And the front door closes.

Then Sebastian Eels says something that makes me freeze to the spot.

"You can come out now," he calls up the stairs. "The coast is clear."

I look at Violet, and her eyes go wide.

Is he calling *her*?

Then we hear another sound—coming from the room next to the study. There's a muffled thud, and then a *thump, thump, thump*. It sounds like someone walking stiffly across the room toward the door.

"Come on!" Violet pulls my arm and we race upstairs to the third-floor landing, just in time. A door opens on the landing below.

Looking over the bannisters, we see a crooked shadow loom across the carpet.

Boat Hook Man.

"You have been very patient, my old friend," says Eels,

heading upstairs to meet him. "Come, please, into my study. We need to discuss tonight's plan."

Peering down from the floor above, we see the writer walk briskly into the book-lined room where Violet and I had been just moments before. The misshapen form of the old mariner sways after him in a cloud of mist, leaving watery footprints on the landing. The door is left open.

"Tonight . . . ?" says Boat Hook Man, in his voice like a far-away wind. "Tonight I will be free?"

"You will," says Eels. "I promise. Tonight I will finish it all, and end your curse. You'll be Captain Kraken again."

"Swear to it!" gusts Boat Hook Man. "Swear!"

"Don't you wave that hook at me," says Eels, with ice in his voice. "Remember how you were when I found you? Nothing more than a foggy patch in that stinking cave—cursed to linger on forever but growing fainter by the year. I'm giving you the chance to make things right again. All you have to do is keep your side of the bargain and fight the monster while I grab the egg."

Boat Hook Man lets out a long, breathy hiss.

"But it is . . . it is . . . invincible."

"You don't have to win, you fool!" Eels shouts. "We've been over all this. You just have to keep the creature busy. Once I have the egg, it will all be over."

"It will kill you," says Boat Hook Man. "Like it killed my crew. My fine, brave men . . ."

"It has a weakness," says Eels. "It *can* be destroyed."

"But . . . this weakness . . . we do not know it."

"If Peter Parma could find it, then so can I," Eels snaps. "It can't be too complicated. He even put it in his stupid book!"

"We have his book . . ." gusts Boat Hook Man, "yet still we do not know."

Even from up here we can hear Eels grinding his teeth.

"Only because Precious Peter removed that page. Curse him!"

"Then we should delay." Boat Hook Man sighs. "Wait till next year. Find . . . the missing page."

"No!" Eels shouts. "I've waited long enough. I *deserve* the egg! I'll be damned if I'm going to let that bleeding-heart Peter stand in my way, even from beyond the grave. We carry on as planned. Once I have the egg, I can use it to find the creature's weakness."

"I thought this too"—Boat Hook Man's voice breaks a little—"all those years ago. But I failed. And was cursed forever."

"Enough of your whining!" Eels brings his fist down on the desk. "It's not my fault you didn't have the wit or the will to use the egg properly. But with its power *I* will be able to know anything, to *do* anything! I'll use that power to destroy the malamander. I'll put a dozen harpoons through its stinking fish guts before it can even spit. Then the egg will be mine forever."

"And . . . the others?" gusts the voice of Boat Hook Man. "If they come . . . to stop you?"

"Oh, don't worry about them." Eels gives a snort of contempt. "I'm not going to let a couple of do-gooders get in my way. I have plenty of harpoons, and the sea will quickly dispose of the bodies."

CHAPTER 27

FEAR AND VAPOR

Suddenly the idea of creeping back downstairs past the study door doesn't seem very appealing. I look at Violet, who is pointing upward.

The third flight of stairs in Sebastian Eels's house is narrower than the others. We creep up and find an attic floor with lower ceilings.

"There must be another way out," Violet whispers, and she pushes open the nearest door. It creaks loudly, and we freeze where we stand. But no angry voice shouts up at us, and the two men remain in the study below, engrossed in their talk of nighttime plans and harpoon guns.

We enter what looks like a small storage room filled with old furniture and crates. There's a small sink in the corner with a dripping tap. Outside the single dormer window, I see the snow-laden tiles of the roof.

"Are you good with heights?" Violet asks.

"Of course," I squeak. "If they're good with me."

Violet heads to the window.

"Wait," I say. "I need to know something first."

"Herbie, what is wrong with you?"

"I—I just need to know that you aren't keeping anything from me."

"Like what?"

"Like"—I tug at my cap—"like who those people are who visited Eels just now. The man and the woman."

"How would I know that?" Violet almost forgets to whisper. Then she stares at me.

"You don't think—?"

"I don't know what to think anymore," I say with a shrug. "But I only have your word for it that you are looking for your parents. It seems to me it's going to be impossible to find them, and yet here you are anyway, poking around in Eels's study and getting involved in our local legends."

Violet's expression is cold and incredulous. For a moment the only sound is the dripping of the tap.

"Poking around?" Violet says at last. She's squared up to

me now and balled her fists. "It's your stupid legends that got involved with *me!*"

I know I'm being unreasonable, but something still doesn't add up. Just then the dripping tap starts to rattle, water sputtering from the spout.

We both turn to it. As we watch, vapor begins to pour out of the tap, billowing into a cloud of mist. But it doesn't move like an ordinary cloud. It gathers instead into a shape — a great, looming shape.

The shape of a man.

"Boat Hook Man?" Violet and I both cry out.

And it's true, no matter how unbelievable it sounds. The mist is rapidly solidifying into the old captain — his vacant eyes, his dripping beard — and the part that is most solid of all is his vicious hook.

"The window!" Violet yells, and she twists the catch, flinging it open.

Boat Hook Man lifts his hook hand high and sweeps it toward me. I drop to the floorboards, and his arm slices through the air where I was just standing, showering me with water.

"You cannot stop us!" he roars like a gathering storm. "I will be free!"

By now Violet is out the window and clinging to the snowy frame.

"Quick, Herbie!"

I jump to my feet, pushing my cap out of my eyes, but Boat Hook Man is between me and the window now, bringing his hook hand up again. I grab something from the nearest crate—an old silver tea tray—and hold it like a shield just as the hook comes crashing down. I see the underside of the tray bulge and split as the hook punctures it. The tray is wrenched from my hand.

The man bellows with fury. I lunge straight for the window, but I don't think I'll make it.

Then something white flashes past me and flies up at Boat Hook Man. It spits and hisses and wraps itself around the man's face. I look back and realize what it is.

"Erwin!"

The cat is attacking the old mariner's head ferociously, raking at him with his claws. But instead of blood, only water spouts from the wounds.

"Come on!" shouts Violet, and I don't need to be told again. I grab her hand and she pulls me out onto the roof—or rather the narrow stretch of roof below the windowsill. The snowy ground four stories below wavers before my eyes.

Boat Hook Man finally gets his hand on Erwin, and the poor cat is flung to one side.

I wish I could do something to help Erwin, but it's all I can do to edge away from the window before Boat Hook Man lunges at it, his face a blank roar, his beard streaming with salt water from his torn face. He thrusts his hook hand forward again, but the tray is still stuck to it, and it catches on the window.

"Don't look down!" says Violet, pulling me farther along, her feet braced against the lead guttering. It bulges with our combined weight. The roof is steep, and the tiles offer no grip whatsoever.

"Where should I look, then?" I gasp as the guttering makes another groan. "Back?"

I give "back" a try and instantly regret it—Boat Hook Man is already climbing out the window, the tray shaken free of his hook.

"The next-door roof looks flatter," says Violet. "And it's only a small jump."

"*Jump?*" I say.

But what choice do we have?

Boat Hook Man is standing on the gutter now, which shrieks and twists as the metal gives under his watery bulk. And I'm not far enough away. He raises his hook hand to strike at me yet again, so I duck . . .

Then something happens that changes everything.

An object flashes over my head.

It's one of Sebastian Eels's steel harpoons.

If I hadn't been ducking at that moment, the harpoon

wouldn't have been flashing over anything, because it would have been going straight through me!

Instead it strikes the roof tiles above with a *CRACK!*, sending up an explosion of snow before ricocheting back . . .

and clonking Boat Hook Man in the face!

The ancient sailor, as surprised as I am by this, clutches at his face with both hand and hook and lets go of the window frame.

And he falls.

I can't turn away, can't not look as the man plunges down, down, down and shatters into a great cloud of swirling vapor and ice particles on the cobbles below.

As the mist whirls away to nothing, I see someone standing there, just beyond the empty man-shaped crater of snow: Sebastian Eels, looking up at us, fury on his face.

And still holding his harpoon gun.

"Now!" shouts Vi, and she runs at the gap
to the next house. Without pausing, she jumps.
She lands, and her feet slide. Leaning forward into the
tiles, she braces against the gutter, and stops.

"Herbie, *come on!*"

I look down again.

Sebastian Eels raises his harpoon gun and takes aim.

I don't even have time to
straighten my cap. I run at the gap
and jump.

It's as I'm sailing through the
frosty air, high above the town of
Eerie-on-Sea, that I see the harpoon
hit Violet.

CHAPTER 28

SILVER-TIPPED

I don't shout. I don't even say the bad word. I'm too shocked. Somehow, on autopilot, I land on the roof and brace myself. The only thing I can see, the only thing I can focus on, is Violet falling back against the roof tiles, the harpoon sticking out of her chest.

"No, no, no . . ." I start yammering. "Violet, no!"

I grab the harpoon and pull it out. There's no blood, but I put my hand on her chest and push down hard before any can start gushing.

"What are you doing?" Violet looks at me, dazed.

I let go, expecting my hands to come away crimson and dripping, but there is still no blood.

"Violet, stay calm. I can get you to Dr. Thalassi. He can do something. They can do amazing things these days, doctors, and—"

Violet reaches into her coat. She pulls out the blue-green volume she was dispensed by the mermonkey. Its cover is pierced with a neat triangular hole, right through the second A in MALAMANDER. She turns it over, and we see a small bulge where the harpoon nearly, but not quite, punctured through the other side.

"If this book had been a page shorter," says Vi, staring, "I wouldn't have lived to finish it."

I'm still holding the harpoon. I see it trembling in my hand. I look down to where Eels was standing, but the man is no longer outside his house.

"He's probably coming up the stairs for a closer shot," says Vi, pulling herself up. "Come on!"

"Come on *where?*" I say.

But before Violet can reply, there's a meow from the apex of the roof.

"Erwin!"

And sure enough, the cat is sitting there, looking only slightly tousled after his encounter with Boat Hook Man.

We manage to climb up to join him, then all three of us

slide down the other side. Without warning, Erwin hops over the edge. Looking over, we are relieved to see the cat standing on a metal balcony just below. And connected to this is an old fire escape.

We reach the bottom of the rusty metal steps, and I'm surprised that no one has called out or challenged us during our descent. Even when we scramble over a garden wall and drop into a neighboring street in front of a startled old man walking a snarly dog, no one shouts. Violet scoops up Erwin, and we hurry away, trying to act as normal as possible, even though my heart is rattling around in my rib cage like a rubber ball, and my legs feel like squids.

"Will we be safe"—Violet gasps—"in the hotel?"

"Dunno," I say. "But where else can we go?"

We stop for a moment to get our breath back.

"I think the place I most want to go right now," says Violet after a moment, "is Jenny Hanniver's bookshop."

I nod.

"We should take Erwin back anyway."

"Thank you, puss," says Vi, giving him a quick kiss on the head as we hurry away. "I hope you didn't get hurt."

Erwin close his eyes and purrs.

✿

When we reach the Eerie Book Dispensary, I'm surprised to find it's closed and all dark inside.

I rattle the door handle, uselessly, before slumping down on the doorstep. Stupidly, I'm still clutching the harpoon.

Violet sits down beside me.

"Did you see . . . ?" she says. "Boat Hook Man! Did he really . . . ?"

I nod.

"Like a ghost," Violet continues. "He came out of the tap like a ghost. I didn't think such things were possible."

I shrug.

"If the impossible is possible anywhere, it'll be possible in Eerie-on-Sea."

Hey, that's quite good, that is. I should say it more often. Then I realize that it wasn't actually me who said it at all. And it wasn't Violet.

We both look at Erwin.

The cat narrows his blue eyes at us and emits a smug purr.

"You heard him that time, right?" Violet says to me. "Herbie, please tell me you just heard Erwin say those words."

"I heard him," I say. Then I turn back to the cat. "Hey, fleabag, you're talking to everyone now, are you?"

Cats don't have eyebrows, but Erwin manages to raise one at me anyway.

"OK, OK, I'm sorry," I say. "'Fleabag' isn't fair. Not after you saved me from Boat Hook Man. But I thought you spoke only to me. I thought we agreed years ago that you'd keep it secret."

Erwin half lowers his eyelids at me and, in a bored human voice, says, "ME-OW."

But the look on his face is all "Oh, no, Herbie Lemon, I didn't agree to any such thing."

Then the cat climbs onto Violet's lap and purrs in exaggerated contentment as she strokes him.

"This town is weird," says Violet in an amazed voice. "Weird, but wonderful."

"Weird and wonderful, yes," I say, "but also dangerous. Thanks again, Erwin."

I give the cat a scratch behind the ear.

"And how about me, Herbie?" says Violet, sticking her chin out. "Still not sure you can trust me? I mean, now that I've been shot and nearly killed by a harpoon, do you still think I'm in cahoots with Sebastian Eels?"

I adjust my cap and nearly meet her eye.

"Um," I say, twiddling that very same harpoon between my fingers. "Sorry about that."

"How could you even think it?"

"It's just . . ." I say. "Vi, how *did* you know where Eels lives?"

Violet's chin wobbles slightly.

"OK," she says. "I suppose I haven't been completely straight with you."

"Oh?"

She folds her arms.

"Look, it took me a long time to pluck up the courage to leave my guardian and come here, Herbie. And I might not have come at all if Great-Aunt Winniegar hadn't decided to start a new life in Tasmania."

"You came here from Tasmania?"

"No!" says Violet. "Tasmania's on the other side of the world. If I'd gone, too, it would have been years before I could have come to Eerie-on-Sea, if ever. But I knew that if I ran away just as we were due to leave, my guardian wouldn't bother trying to find me. She'd never risk missing her boat, and that new life she wanted would certainly be happier without me getting in the way."

Erwin arches his back and rubs Violet's cheek with his head.

"Anyway," says Vi, "it also meant I had less time to prepare than I thought, less time to research Eerie-on-Sea. Almost all the information I could find was about Sebastian Eels."

"Eels?"

"Yes. He's more famous than you might realize, Herbie. My

local library has lots of his books. Even Great-Aunt Winniegar has read some. So when I got here, I honestly thought he would be my main lead to my parents. I imagined, since my dad is an author too, that Eels would have known him, that they would have been friends. It's what gave me the idea to come here in the first place."

"But I thought you said you came to see me?" I say, though I hate the whiny tone it brings to my voice. "You said you needed a detective, that you needed my lost-and-foundering to solve the case. You said *I* was famous."

"Oh, Herbie, I *do* need you. I didn't lie. It's just that I'd never met you, and the hotel sounded so strange when I read about it, and I was nervous about coming to such a grand old place. I didn't know how you'd react. So, instead, when I arrived at the railway station, I asked someone the way to Sebastian Eel's house, and they told me, simple as that. I went there—just to look at first—but when I saw that a back window was open, I thought, well, I thought . . ."

"You thought you'd start the adventure without me."

"Don't say it like that," says Violet with a groan. "Anyway, I had a good look over the house, which I thought was empty, and found the study. I was just about to get down to some serious rummaging when I realized there was someone there."

"Eels?" I say, but Violet shakes her head and shudders.

"No, worse. Imagine how it felt to be in a stranger's house, without permission, in the dark, and see Boat Hook Man emerging from the shadows. It was terrifying."

"That's when you came to the hotel?"

Violet nods.

"I tried to lose him. I ran and I ran, but he was faster than I would have ever imagined. I couldn't shake him off. I didn't know where else to go."

"And that's it?" I say. "That's all you are keeping from me?"

"Yes, I promise," Violet says. "I should have told you sooner. I just thought you'd get the wrong idea if you knew where I'd been and what I'd been doing, and I was right, wasn't I?"

I say nothing. I lift my eyes to the glass tower of the Grand Nautilus Hotel, peering like an eye over the roofs and eaves of the old town. Lady Kraken can see a lot with that cameraluna of hers, but seeing isn't necessarily understanding. No wonder she needs someone like me on the ground. For a moment I'm tempted to wave up at her. Then it crosses my mind to make a rude sign. In the end, though, I just get to my feet and brush the snow off my bottom.

"I'm starving," I say. "Let's go to Seegol's for chips. We need to figure out what to do next."

"Good idea," says Vi, standing too.

Erwin strolls over to the door of the book dispensary and meows, pawing at the door.

"I'm sorry, puss, but it's locked," says Vi, and she rattles the handle to show him. "You'll just have to wait for Jenny to—"

Then she stops.

We both stare openmouthed as the door, which I swear was locked fast a moment ago, swings quietly open.

CHAPTER 29

THE ACHILLES' SPOT

It's dark inside the book dispensary. The fire is cold in the hearth, and the only light comes from the tall bay window.

"Hello?" I call.

There's no answer.

"We really shouldn't be in here," says Vi, hesitating in the doorway.

"Ha!" I reply. "Says the girl who breaks into people's houses all the time. Besides, it kind of feels as if Erwin has invited us in. This is his home, too. I don't think Jenny would mind."

As if to confirm this, Erwin jumps into one of the armchairs and curls up. But I cannot help noticing that he keeps one of his eyes open, watching us.

Violet walks over to the mermonkey, and I join her. The creature leers down at us over its black typewriter, its hairy shoulders hunched, its ancient battered top hat extended for the offering. There's a slight waft of burned hair and spent fuses around it.

"Thinking of asking it what we should do next?" I say. "People do that, you know. Ask it for guidance. But you have to be careful."

"What do you mean?" says Violet.

"Well, you never know if the book it dispenses will tell you something about your future, or something about your past. Or something else entirely. I met a man once who swears he belched in front of the mermonkey and got dispensed a copy of *Gone with the Wind*, so it definitely has a sense of humor, too."

Violet shrugs.

"It doesn't feel like the moment for a new book," she says. "I'm still working through the last one."

"You're probably right," I say. "Anyway, did you find anything interesting in Eels's study?"

"Yes, my dad's manuscript! His unpublished book about the malamander. It was just lying there on the desk! Eels must have stolen it from my parents' luggage, as we thought. But there's a page missing. Eels has stuck notes all over the pages next to it, trying to figure out what was on that missing part. But it doesn't look as if he could do it."

"That missing page must be pretty important," I say, remembering the conversation we overheard from the study.

"Eels said it was the page where my dad described the malamander's one weakness," says Violet. "The gap in its armor that he will need to know about if he's going to be sure of killing it and keeping the egg."

"Then your dad did the right thing by taking it out!" I say. "I can't believe he put in something like that."

"He probably couldn't help himself," says Violet. "From all I've heard, I think my dad loved the old stories too much. I expect he couldn't bear to leave anything out. In the end, though, he must have known it was a mistake and hid the page somewhere. Maybe he sensed danger from Eels. Thank goodness he did."

"It sounds as though Eels is crazy enough to try to steal the egg anyway," I say. "So hopefully the big bully will get himself eaten by the monster, and the rest of us can live happily ever after."

"I won't, though, will I?" she says with a sigh. "I still won't know what happened to my mum and dad."

I nod. What can I say to that? Then I think of something. . . .

"Let's go get those chips."

I turn and head toward the shop door. But I see that Violet hasn't moved.

"Herbie, do you remember what Jenny said about my dad's last visit to the book dispensary?" she asks. "The time he brought my mum?"

"Yeah," I say. "She said he wanted to show the mermonkey to your mother. And that he had his manuscript with him."

"But there was something else," says Violet. "Don't you remember? Jenny said Dad was goofing around with the mermonkey's hat, trying it on."

I shrug. Why is that important? But then . . .

"Hey, wait—what are you doing?" I blurt out, because Violet has just tugged the mermonkey's top hat right out of its hand! The mermonkey shivers, and a few dead flies fall to the floor, but the creature remains inactive.

Violet raises the crumbling hat with both hands, as if about to put it on, even though there's no way it would go over her mass of curls. Then she lowers it again and peers inside.

"Vi, you should put that back," I say. "Jenny won't mind us being in her shop, but she will mind very much if we break the mermonkey. You heard what she said about your dad always having to fix it."

But Violet just peers even closer into the fusty old hat.

"I did hear," she says. "I heard that he even patched up this very hat, though the band inside is loose, and the lining is coming out. . . ."

"The whole cronky apparatus must be a hundred years old, at least." I start hopping from one foot to the other as I watch Violet poking her finger into the lining of the hat. "Vi, please be careful!"

"There seems to be something here," she says. "Something behind the band . . ."

And she pulls out a small square of folded paper.

Violet looks at me. Her eyes go wide.

I clutch my cap.

"No way!" I say. "Is that . . . ?"

Then we both speak at once.

"The missing page!"

Violet shoves the hat back into the mermonkey's hand and unfolds the paper. Sure enough, it's a page from a typed manuscript. At the top is a title, as if it's the start of a new chapter.

"*The Achilles' Spot,*" says Violet, reading the title aloud. Then she starts to read the rest:

> "*Now we come to the matter of the malamander's fabled weakness, the one vulnerability that renders the otherwise invincible monster all too vincible. We have already seen, in*

previous chapters, that many of the oldest accounts of the malamander legend allude to this so-called 'Achilles' Spot,' without ever describing it. However, I intend to break with tradition and set out plainly that the malamander's one vulnerability is . . ."

Violet stops reading. A shadow has been thrown across the page. We both look up.

"Well, don't stop there," says Sebastian Eels from the doorway of the book dispensary. "You were just getting to the good bit."

CHAPTER 30

THE MISSING PAGE

The writer looks only slightly disheveled in his expensive suit, his mop of dark hair only a little out of place. Not at all like a man who has just shot two harpoons — one at me and one at Violet — and shot them both to kill. His sudden reappearance is so shocking that Violet and I just stand there, transfixed. Which is why Eels is able to snatch the paper from her so easily.

"Well, well, the missing page," he says, straightening his tie. "And just as I'd given up hope of ever finding it."

"No!" cries Violet. "That's not yours, it's my *dad's* . . ."

She tries to snatch the paper back, but Eels picks her up. Just like that—he picks her up with one hand and throws her out of his way. Violet lands, stumbling, and falls back into an armchair.

In an instant, Erwin flies at Eels, hissing as he claws up his legs and sinks his teeth into the man's hand, making him drop the paper.

"Little weasel!" cries Eels, flinging Erwin away. The cat twists in the air, ready to land on all fours, but he hits the corner of a bookshelf and instead falls limply to the ground.

And me? Well, I've grabbed the paper, haven't I? But then there's a clonk to end all clonks as Eels brings his fist down on my head. My Lost-and-Founder's cap is forced over my eyes, and I go down.

It's a moment before I can find up again. When I do, I see that Eels is towering over me. I look over at Violet. She's still in the chair, clutching her throat. Erwin is in her arms now, trembling with pain.

"The Achilles' Spot," Eels reads aloud to us from the paper, as if he's giving a lecture. "Of course, you both know who Achilles was."

He glances at each of us in turn.

"No? Well, then, allow me to remind you. The hero Achilles was dipped in the magical River Styx as a baby, and his body was made invulnerable all over. All over, that is, except at the place where his mother held him for the dipping. In the case of Achilles, his heel was his weakness. And it was an arrow in the heel that brought about his death many years later. But let's see where the malamander's Achilles' spot is. . . ."

Eels stops taunting us and reads the rest of the page, his lips moving quickly and silently with the words. Then he gasps. His gasp becomes a snort of derisive laughter.

"Is this some kind of joke?" the man says eventually, his brows lowering and his eyes going dark. "Is this all I have to do to kill the monster?"

"You're the monster!" cries Violet. "I hope the malamander bites your head off."

"Well, that *was* a distinct possibility," says Eels, tapping the paper lightly. "But now that I know this . . . well, who'd have thought it? Who'd have thought that such a fearsome, armored fiend as the malamander—a monster that destroyed a whole battleship and its crew—would have such a soft heart?"

"What do you mean?" I say, despite myself. "Soft heart?"

"I suppose there's no harm in telling you," says Eels, refolding the sheet of paper and sliding it into his jacket. "According to dear Peter, the monster opens its heart when it lays its egg. Quite literally—the armored plates over its heart fold back so that its beatings can be heard in the ocean. That's how it calls its mate. On the coldest, darkest night of the year, the malamander lays its poor lonesome heart bare to summon its long-lost mate home to the nest. And doesn't it just make you want to puke? How pathetic! But also, how very unsurprising that a softy like Peter Parma would be the one to discover such a ridiculous fact."

"My dad is a great man!" cries Violet. "He's greater than you'll ever be."

"Is?" says Eels. "I think you mean *was*. Please don't tell me that you actually think your parents are still alive. Ah, but I see from your face that you do. Oh, dear. Well, it hardly matters now. But I'll tell you what. Once I have the malamander egg, and can make my every wish come true, I promise you, Violet Parma, that I'll wipe you out of existence and end your misery for good!"

And with a snarl, he swings away to the door. Then stops and swings back.

"Oh, I'll be needing this," he says, and stoops to pick up the dropped harpoon, which I'd still been holding when he came in.

"Tempered steel with a silver tip," he says, turning the harpoon in the little light from the window and making it flash cold and bright. "These things cost a fortune. But I need only one tonight, when I destroy the malamander. I'll try to make it this one."

CHAPTER 31

PETER PARMA'S MAGNUM OPUS

I t's all my fault!" Violet puts her head in her hands.

We're sitting in Seegol's steamy diner, which is surprisingly busy. The clatter of knives and forks and the murmur of locals drowns out the sound of Violet's despair, which is probably just as well.

"If I hadn't been meddling in all this, Eels would never have found that page!"

Seegol arrives at that moment.

"But what is this? Tears at lunchtime? This is not good."

I've already scattered the contents of my coat pocket across the table. I think about doing the speech again, but Seegol knows the drill by now.

"It's been a tricky day," I tell him. "Could we have something to cheer us up . . . for *this*?"

And I slide over a small silver and cut-glass cigarette lighter that has been in the Lost-and-Foundery since before the First World War. No one will be coming for it now.

"For this you can have the works," declares Seegol, and he pats Violet on the shoulder before heading off to his kitchen island to drop fish in the fryer.

"You mustn't beat yourself up, Vi," I say, leaning forward so only she can hear. "There's still no guarantee that Eels will succeed. According to the stories, people have been trying to take the malamander's egg since forever, and no one has managed it yet. Even Captain Kraken, who had a small army to fight for him, couldn't keep it for long. The malamander will kill Sebastian Eels, and it'll be his own stupid fault."

Violet's face reappears from inside her hair.

"And its weakness?"

I open my mouth to speak, but then I close it again. I had been going to say that Eels would have to be a crack shot to hit a precise opening in the malamander's armor, but then I remember the targets in his house. The bull's-eyes were riddled with holes.

"And what about my parents?" Violet continues. "I came here to find them, but instead all I've done is ruin everything. Maybe it's time I accept that they are nowhere to be found. Maybe it's time I accept they were probably killed by the malamander too."

"Vi . . ."

"We both know it's possible!" Violet cries. "It's certainly more likely than them just strolling into this diner, alive and well, after all these years."

We fall silent.

Then we both look over to the door, because, well, in Eerie-on-Sea you never quite know.

But no one comes in.

"This isn't a story, Violet," I say gently, though I hate saying it. "There isn't always a happy ending in real life. Maybe we just have to learn to accept that."

"Even in a town where a two-hundred-year-old sailor can materialize out of a tap and a cat can talk?"

"Not even then," I reply, relieved to see the fish and chips arrive.

"Anyway," I say, after a long pause during which many chips are eaten (mostly by me), "I'm the real ninny here. To think that I had your dad's manuscript in my Lost-and-Foundery all that time, in his luggage, and I never realized what I had!"

"You weren't supposed to know, Herbie."

"Eels must have figured out where it would be," I say. "And I'll bet it was old Mollusc who helped him get it."

"Perhaps, but it was you who kept it safe till then."

I make a face. I still feel like a complete dunderbrain.

"That's your job, Herbie," says Vi, with passion. "And you're brilliant at it. Keeping lost things safe, detecting clues, finding rightful owners. You're amazing, Herbie Lemon. And I'm so glad I met you. . . ."

I chomp another chip and beam.

Well, I suppose I *am* quite amazing.

"But now, finally, I know what *my* job is," Violet goes on, touching the angry scabs on her cheek. "I may not know how to find my parents, but I do know how to fix the mess I've made. I have to stop Sebastian Eels from getting the malamander's egg. I have to face the monster myself."

A wave chooses that moment to hit the pier, sending the salt and pepper shakers rattling across the table.

⚙O✿

It's some time later, and lunch is finished. We're standing outside on the pier, keeping a little warmth from the diner snug inside our big coats as we look over the heaving sea.

The pier shudders again, creaking in the wind that billows and buffets around us. We're standing right at the end of it, on the shriveled wooden planks beyond the old theater. The theater opens only for a month or two in the summer, and looking up at it now, I'm surprised it even does that. It looks like one well-aimed superwave would sweep it into the sea forever.

"So, you're sure about this?" I say to Violet, pointing toward the rising sea. "You're sure about *that*?"

Ahead, the dark green-smeared iron hull of the battleship *Leviathan* is about to vanish beneath the surging waves. Only the two great chimneys—corroded almost to collapse—and one gun turret are still visible as the tide climbs to claim them again.

"The malamander hibernates," Violet tells me. "I saw that in my dad's manuscript; although, it was probably my mum who figured it out. It sleeps for part of the year, somewhere far out in the ocean, the whole summer long, but then, when winter hits, it comes near the town to hunt, and to lay its egg on Midwinter night."

"In the wreck?" I say, and Violet nods.

"My dad must have come out here to watch it. My mum too. When the tide was low enough."

"As it will be later tonight . . ." I say.

"And then, when its mate doesn't come, the poor thing devours its own egg and swims away alone, to wait another year."

"Poor thing."

Violet shrugs.

"The malamander has lost its mate. I've lost my parents. It's funny to have something in common with a monster, but I do." Then, after a pause, Violet adds, "And I wonder if you do too, Herbie."

"Me?"

"Well, I can't help noticing," says Violet, turning to me, "that you don't seem to have any parents either."

I pick a large flake of rust off the pier railing and pretend to find it interesting. I'm a castaway with no memory, washed up on a strange shore in a crate of lemons and adopted by a whole town. But Violet is wrong. She was lost, yes, but I was found. It isn't the same thing at all.

"Herbie?"

"I'll tell you my story one day, Vi," I say, flicking the rust flake into the sea. "I promise. But first, we have work to do."

"We?"

"Of course *we*. You don't think I'm going to let you finish the adventure without me, do you?"

"But, Herbie, it'll be extremely dangerous. . . ."

"All the more reason for me to come with you," I say, setting my cap straight and standing tall. "You handed yourself in at *my* Lost-and-Foundery, Violet Parma, and I'm not letting you get lost again. I took on your case, and I'm going to see it through."

The wind ruins the moment by pushing my cap back down over my face, but Violet doesn't seem to notice. She throws her arms around me in a huge hug. Then she looks a bit embarrassed and tries to hide it by punching me on the arm. So I try to pretend it doesn't hurt, until the soppy moment has passed.

"We need to get back to the Lost-and-Foundery and get ready,"
I say, when it has. "There's loads of stuff there we can use."

"Thanks, Herbie."

"Don't thank me yet," I say. "Thank me when we're toasting
crumpets tomorrow morning, laughing at stupid old Sebastian
Eels and how we stopped him in his tracks."

And so we set off back along the pier, toward the lights of
the Grand Nautilus Hotel.

CHAPTER 32

DODGY BUSINESS

When we get back to the hotel, Violet heads for the side passage so I can let her in through the cellar window. I call her back.

"Not this time," I say. "I think you should come through the front door like everyone else."

"Won't they see me in Reception?" asks Violet.

"Seriously?" I look at her. "After everything we've been through, you're worried about that?"

"But won't I get *you* into trouble?"

I look at her some more.

"Er, you've been getting me into trouble ever since you got here, remember?"

So we walk up the steps and through the great double doors of the Grand Nautilus Hotel, side by side.

It's as we're lifting the counter in my cubbyhole that Mr. Mollusc sees us.

"Herbert Lemon!" He strides over, bristling his small mustache. "It is not permitted to take guests down there. Please attend to the young lady in the correct manner and . . ."

Then he stops, probably because now he has a good view of Violet. I try to imagine what he sees: a wild-haired girl with a scratched face, in a too-big borrowed coat and a ratty pullover. A girl with a harpoon hole through her clothes, and her mother's boots clogged with sand and seaweed. I see the vein start to throb on his temple, right on cue.

"What is the meaning of this?" the hotel manager hisses, lowering his voice in case any of his precious guests are nearby.

"Violet's a friend," I say. "There's nothing in the rules to say I can't have a friend over."

Mr. Mollusc grinds his teeth as he jabs his finger at me.

"I don't understand what you're even doing here, boy. Didn't Her Ladyship fire you this morning?"

"Fire me?" I chortle. "Lady Kraken didn't fire me. In fact, she asked me to do her a special favor. She asked me to keep my eyes open for any dodgy business going on in her hotel."

"But . . ." Mollusc is quivering with rage now. "*You* are the dodgy business in this hotel, Lemon! YOU!"

"I think she had something else in mind," I say, straightening my cap and fixing the man with my best stare. "Like, for instance, someone stealing things from my Lost-and-Foundery."

"Stealing?" Mr. Mollusc says, the first hint of doubt creeping into his voice.

"Yeah, stealing." I dial the stare up a notch or two. "I mean, going down into my basement when I'm not there, taking suitcases that don't belong to you, and then signing them out as if collected by family. *That* sort of stealing."

Mr. Mollusc passes his hand though his wispy hair. There is suddenly a bead of sweat in his horrible mustache.

"Oh, I see." He forces a smile. "Why would anyone do such a thing . . . ?"

"For money, I expect," says Violet. "The worst reason of all."

Old Mollusc looks from one of us to the other, his mouth opening and closing like a fish's.

"I should think that if Lady Kraken were to sack someone," I say, quite loudly now, so that everyone in the reception lobby can hear, "it would be someone who'd done a really bad thing like that. Wouldn't you agree?"

"Very well, very well." Mollusc waves his hands to shush me. "Very well, Lemon. Carry on as you were. No need to make a fuss."

"It's MISTER Lemon, actually," I say, and he gives me a look of desperate fury.

"Mr. Lemon. Quite so."

And with that, the hotel manager walks away, slightly wobbly, and locks himself in the lavatory.

In my cellar we stoke up the fire and settle down to wait for night. But no time at all later, Violet looks out the window and announces that the night is already here.

CHAPTER 33

WILL-O'-THE-SEA-WISP

"Maybe we should tell someone what we're planning to do," I say.

"Maybe," Violet replies, "but who would we tell? Who can we trust?"

"Jenny Hanniver," I say. "I trust Jenny. And I think Dr. Thalassi's all right, really."

Violet looks at me.

"And what if they try to stop us? If they do, Eels could get the egg. What then?"

I don't have an answer to that.

Violet climbs back into her coat, warm now, and then pulls on her mother's boots. I go through some of the baskets of loose lost stuff and pull out two hefty flashlights. Batteries are a bit harder to find, but I get both flashlights working.

As soon as we think they are hot enough, we take a couple of pebbles each from the top of the wood burner, one for each pocket. We scarf down the remainder of my leftover sandwiches.

"We'll both leave this way," I say then, opening the cellar window into the night. "It will be better if everyone in the hotel thinks we're still down here."

And with that we climb out.

<O>

It's as cold as ever in the old seaside town. A wind like the breath of ice dragons hits us as we cross the snowy cobbles to the sea-wall. The pier is nothing but a series of small swaying lights leading to the snug inviting glow of Seegol's Diner. Above which, in light-bulb letters, the words EERIE-ON-SEA fizz and flicker in the frigid air. But we aren't going to the pier. When we look down over the beach, we can see next to nothing.

"Tide's already out," says Violet, leading the way down the worn stone steps to the sand.

The surface of the beach has a crust of ice. It takes a lot to freeze seawater, but believe me, here in Eerie we have what it takes, and then some. We crunch our way out to the sea along the iron legs of the pier, the small lights of the town twinkling as they fall behind. Once we draw level with Seegol's Diner — a last outpost of friendly warmth on the pier above — we are faced with the great void of nothingness beyond.

"Should we use our flashlights?" Violet shouts above the wind. "They'd be useful but also a giveaway. Eels would see us coming a mile off."

"It's tempting," I call back. "I can't even see ten paces ahead, let alone all the way to the wreck, but I think we should let our eyes adapt, if they can."

So we head on into the dark, sticking close together, hearing the wind whistling in the pier struts to our left, until even that is gone.

"Can you see anything?" I shout into Violet's ear. The wind has become a roar.

I feel her shake her head.

"Except . . ." she says. "What's that?"

"What?" I reply.

"That light. Over there. A purple light."

I squint over to where I think Violet is pointing. A purple light?

And then I see it. A small point of light that bobs along like a will-o'-the-wisp, farther up the beach, reflected faintly on the wet sand. And, yes, *purple.*

"OK, that's weird," I say. "I . . . I don't know what that is."

"Whatever it is, it's getting closer. Should we run?"

"Yes!" I shout, and we do, heading straight out toward the sea as fast as we can on the crusty sand. The purple light bobs a moment longer, then flashes, as if it has seen us and wants a closer look.

" . . . LOOOOO!" comes a sound, hardly reaching us over the wind. "HALLOOOOOO!"

I grab Violet's arm and pull her to a stumbling halt.

"HALLOOOO!" I cry back, cupping my hands around my mouth.

"What is it?" says Violet, gasping.

"Not *what*," I say with a grin. "*Who*. Look!"

And a figure steps forward into near visibility, just ahead of us. The purple light flashes up and picks out the features of a face we both know, muffled by several scarfs and topped off with at least three hats, tied on with string.

"Mrs. Fossil!" I cry. "Are we glad to see you. We thought we were about to be abducted by sea fairies or something."

"Herbie, what are you doing out here?" puffs Mrs. Fossil as she reaches us. "Don't you know it's the longest and darkest night of the year?"

"We could ask you the same question," says Violet. "How's your arm?"

"Oh, it's not so bad," says Mrs. F. "A bit stiff, but I can still hold a bucket. It's certainly not bad enough to stop me from amber hunting."

"Amber hunting?" Violet and I say together.

"Ah, maybe you don't know," says the beachcomber, waving her purple light around. "Amber glows under ultraviolet light. It's hard to spot in the daytime, but at night it shines out a treat when I flash my UV light on it. Look!"

And she pulls a handful of something out of her coat pocket and shines the purple light down onto it. We huddle around. There, in her palm, are several small stones, glowing faintly green in the ultraviolet.

"It's the best time of the year for finding it," she says, clutching her hats against the wind. "Ancient tree sap, as I'm sure you know. I once found a piece with a millipede in it, as big as your . . ."

"Mrs. Fossil," I say, jumping in before the story starts, "we'd love to see that. Maybe we can come by tomorrow. But right now, we're wondering if you have seen anyone else out here. On the beach. Someone heading for the wreck of the *Leviathan*, perhaps?"

"For the wreck?" says Mrs. F. "Surely no one would be that stupid. The tide may be low now, but it'll rise again like a flood. Anyone foolish enough to be in that old wreck would be drowned in a jiffy."

"Thanks," I say. I manage to catch Violet's eye, despite the dark, and realize that our eyes *are* adapting, after all.

"Aren't you scared, Mrs. Fossil?" asks Violet. "To be out here in the dark, I mean. After what happened to you."

I can just make out Mrs. F's topmost hat shaking from side to side.

"The way I see it, I was unlucky to get bitten last time. As long as I steer clear of rock pools, I reckon I'll be fine. And I can't resist these little beauties!" She waves her palmful of gems at us again.

"Even so," says Violet, "maybe you should call it a night. You've got some great amber there. Wouldn't you like to go back to your wonderful shop and put the kettle on?"

"That sounds like a splendid idea." Mrs. F's teeth flash purple-white in the UV light. "Would you two like to join me? I have scones."

"We'd love to, but there's something we have to do first," I say, steering Violet away. "Good night, Mrs. F!"

"Wait, I'm not sure I should leave you here," Mrs. Fossil calls hesitantly from behind us. "Why are you out on the beach, Herbie? In the dark?"

"It's just lost-luggage business," I call back. "Herbie Lemon and Violet Parma are on the case, if you see what I mean, ha-ha!"

And we disappear into the night.

"Wait!" comes the fading voice of Mrs. Fossil. "Wait, what did you say? Parma? Did you say Violet *Parma?*"

But we don't wait to talk anymore, and soon the wind has swallowed up Mrs. Fossil's words.

CHAPTER 34

WARSHIP

··

It's only when we splash into water that we stop.

"Herbie, we really need to use the flashlights," says Vi, leaning in close again to make herself heard. "What if we walk right out to sea?"

But I hold up a nearly invisible hand.

"Wait a sec," I say. "Look up at the clouds."

A patch of lightness in the northern sky, which I'd had my eye on for a while now, finally opens — ripped apart by the wind — and the moon shines down in a rush of silver.

The wreck is shockingly close. Its jagged outline towers up just a few dozen paces ahead of us. Water swirls around it, crashing in waves against its far side before surging around each end and sweeping over the beach toward us, covering the sand—and our feet—in icy-cold sea.

"I thought the tide was going out," Violet shouts in my ear.

"It is," I shout back. "I checked at Reception. It'll be out completely at 10:13 p.m." And I pull back my sleeve to waggle the glowing dial of my watch—borrowed from lost property, of course—at Violet. "That's in twenty-seven minutes."

"So we just stand here till then?" Violet says, through chattering teeth.

I shrug. I haven't actually thought this far ahead in detail. Deciding to stop Eels from getting the egg is one thing. Actually doing it? Well, that's something else, isn't it? And we're already frozen through.

"What's that?" Violet points back up the beach. The town is just a mass of misty lights, twinkling in the distance. But down at shore level is another light—a small speck, sharper than the others, that is swinging from side to side. And getting closer.

"Maybe it's Mrs. Fossil," I say, "coming back to insist on that scone."

I'm starting to wish we'd gone with her after all.

"I don't think so," says Violet. "Herbie, what if it's Eels?"

"If it is, he'll see us," I say. "Now that the moon's out."

"Then let's go," Violet replies. "Let's get to the wreck before he does."

HMS *Leviathan* must have been a monster in its day. Almost as long as the pier, and twice as wide, it was probably an awesome sight as it crested the waves. Now, though, it's the waves that crest *it*. Most of the ship's hull is submerged in the silt and sands of the bay. The deck is partly exposed, however, from the middle section forward, sweeping up at a drunken angle, bristling with gun turrets, twisted metal railings, and barnacle-encrusted structures. All of it dripping with seaweed and slime. The prow—the pointy end, that is—rises up to be almost the highest part of the wreck, and it is still wrapped around the spur of rock that tore open the hull and sank the mighty warship. The wind gusts over it all with a high metallic wail.

"There must be a way in through there," says Vi, pointing to the split metal of the prow.

"There is," I tell her.

"You've been inside?" Violet looks surprised. "Why didn't you say so?"

"I haven't been *inside*," I say. "I've just been out to look at it a few times. Have you any idea how dangerous this wreck is?"

"My dad's been inside," says Violet. "And Eels. And goodness knows how many others. And we'll have to, too, if we're going to do what we came to do."

"Yeah, I know," I say quickly. "But the tide, Vi. When it comes back in . . ."

"We'll just have to be careful," Violet replies firmly, and I can tell that nothing is going to stop her. "Eels will be here in a moment. Come on!"

"Wait," I say. "If we go in now, Eels will be between us and the way out."

"Well, what, then?"

"Let's see if we can get up on the deck," I say. "I want to watch what Eels does. And if he goes in, we'll have the advantage when we follow."

So we run, splashing in the swirling shallows, till we reach the monstrous black hull. I put my hand on it and feel the faint warmth of my body sucked out into its freezing metal skin.

"We can get up here," says Violet, and I see her silhouetted figure rise ahead of me. I wonder for a moment how she's doing this, till I spot in the moonlight a series of holes corroded through the hull, acting like a ladder.

But the moonlight worries me. Can we be seen already? I look around, and the light on the beach is surprisingly close now. I can even see the shape of a man behind it. It's Eels, there's no mistake, and lumbering behind him is the hulking form of someone else I recognize.

Boat Hook Man.

I glance at Violet, and she's waving at me to hurry. She's

already on the deck of the *Leviathan*. I climb till I can haul myself over onto the deck beside her.

Where I land with a loud metallic *CLANG*!

The approaching light, which had been heading for the prow of the ship, immediately swings around toward us.

We drop low behind the ship's side, but it's riddled with holes, and particles of flashlight beam play over us both.

Violet jabs her finger toward the prow, and I follow her, still crouched. After a moment, we risk another peek.

Sebastian Eels is now walking straight toward the place where we climbed, his flashlight fixed on that point.

"Oh, bladderwracks!" I say, but Violet is pointing again.

Behind us, on the deck, looms one of *Leviathan*'s gun turrets, its two long barrels festooned with dripping seaweed. We manage to duck behind it just as Sebastian Eels swings himself up onto the deck.

The man is an extraordinary sight. He has a full wet suit on, complete with air tank. A diving mask is around his neck, and a mouthpiece dangles at his side, ready for use. Over his suit he wears a long-sleeved shirt of glittering steel chain mail, the kind people wear to swim with sharks. He has a packed equipment belt, a long dagger in a sheath strapped to one thigh, and lights mounted on his helmet. In his hands he holds the harpoon gun, sweeping it from side to side, ready to release its deadly darts at anything he wishes.

We shrink back into the shadow of the gun turret.

There's a porthole door at the back of it, fixed open a sliver on rust-blistered hinges, but do we really dare go in there? I shake my head at Violet when she points at the door. I feel my insides go watery at the thought of what could be lurking inside the turret.

But as we creep around the other side, away from Eels, a dark shadow grows behind us, blotting out the silver moonlight. We spin around and see a terrible sight: Boat Hook Man is hauling himself over the far side of the ship! We're surrounded!

Violet pulls me back toward the door of the turret. I try to shake her off, to protest, but she pulls even harder. Boat Hook Man could swing his head our way any moment and we'll be seen. And Eels is heading around the other way. I let myself be pulled to the twisted metal doorway and watch with mounting horror as Violet squeezes herself through.

Into the dark.

And I have no choice.

As the sound of ringing footsteps grows closer and closer on the iron deck, I edge toward the doorway and allow Violet to pull me into the black, dripping, windowless unknown.

CHAPTER 35

THE MALAMANDER'S LAIR

The stink of the sea is overwhelming.

I shrink back into the darkness, still pulled by Violet, desperately hoping it *is* Violet pulling me and not some flubbery faceless horror from the deep.

"Quiet," I hear her say close to my ear.

It's possible that I'm making some small whimpering sounds right now. I can't, despite my best efforts, stop thinking that very soon the sea will surge back over the deck of the ship and fill this small dark space with water. What if we're still here when that happens? What if the door slams shut? What if this is our . . . tomb?

"Herbie, seriously, be quiet!"

I clench my teeth firmly together.

It's hard to distinguish any sound from outside now, beyond the whistle of the wind. But is that a footstep? Then there's a clang of metal banging against metal, and suddenly, before we can do anything, there's a blinding flash.

A head—it must be Eels's—looks into the doorway, and his head lamps fill the inside of the turret with brilliant light. In a moment of vivid awfulness, I see the slimy metal interior of the turret crawling with sea creatures, and then the light is gone, leaving me blinded, with the memory of those sea creatures swarming in my mind.

Amazingly, Eels doesn't seem to have spotted us. We're flat against one side of the turret, partly shielded by a curtain of seaweed. And he only glanced inside, anyway, perhaps thinking no one in their right mind would crawl into such a small and dismal hole.

"It's not here" we hear him call over the wind, somewhere outside on the deck. "We mustn't waste time . . ."

Another sound cuts through his voice—a high roaring shriek, like sheet metal being rent in two. But it's not really that. In the fetid dark, Violet and I look at each other as we recognize the cry of the malamander.

"Come on!" cries Eels, and we hear his boots thudding away across the deck. Soon we can hear nothing but the gusting of the wind outside.

"I need to get out of here," I whisper, but Violet grabs my arm again.

"Wait! Didn't you notice it?" she says. "When he shone his light inside?"

"It?" I say, remembering the crawling, spiny, scaly creatures that call this watery hell their home. "We need to get out of here, Violet. Now!"

But Violet turns on her flashlight, and the inside of the turret is lit again. The creatures writhe, creeping over my shoes, and I kick them off frantically. But with a longer, more stable light, I also get a sense of the interior of the turret as a space where men once worked, manning the gun. It calms me a bit to think of that, and I manage to brush a lobster off my leg with only a small whimper. And then I notice that Violet is shining her flashlight on something specific.

It's an opening in the floor of the turret. A round opening, with metal foot and hand holds descending down into the belly of the ship.

"It's another way in," she says, picking a shrimp out of her hair and releasing it into a pool. "We could use it to get ahead of Eels."

"And then what?" I say. "Violet, we don't have a plan for this part."

"Something tells me my mum and dad didn't have much of a plan either, but we have to stop Eels from getting the egg, or their sacrifice will have been for nothing."

I groan. She always has an answer I can't argue against. An image of Mrs. Fossil's cozy shop interior comes into my mind, complete with buttered scones and sweet tea, but I shake it away.

"Come on, then," I say with a sigh.

"Thank you for coming with me, Herbie."

"Yeah, whatever," I say. "Just lead the way before we're eaten alive by starfish or something."

Violet loops the strap of her flashlight over one of her coat buttons. With both her hands free, she begins her descent. I take out my own flashlight and do the same. Then I follow her down.

The iron rungs are freezing to the touch, and my sense of claustrophobia grows sharper still as we climb down the metal tube. There's a place where the iron is corroded to nothing, and I have to reach down beyond it with my foot to find the next secure rung. Inside the hole made by the corrosion, an octopus—vivid red-orange—slaps one tentacle against the wall and fixes me with a watery black eye.

"Please tell me we're nearly there," I gasp down the tube to Violet.

"Just a bit farther," she says.

And then my foot is dangling. I've reached the bottom rung, and I splash down into a corridor as silently as I can.

We're deep in the ship now, at the waterline. Our feet are submerged in the bone-freezing sea, and I curse the fact that no one in the Grand Nautilus Hotel has ever lost a pair of waterproof Wellington boots, size six, with a nice fuzzy lining. I untie my flashlight and shine it at my watch.

"Seventeen minutes till low tide," I murmur to Vi, amazed that it's been only ten minutes since I last looked at my watch. "At that point there'll be a bit of time when the water does nothing — they call it slack water — and then it'll be rushing back in here. We have to be gone by then."

And that's when we hear it again: the cry of the malamander — a piercing, shrieking prehistoric sound that echoes through the dripping iron carcass of the battleship.

"That sounds close," I gasp, clutching Violet's arm.

"That's because this is its home," Violet whispers. "Eels might feel confident while the tide is out, with his harpoons and chain mail, but once this place fills with water again, I don't think he'll stand much chance against a monstrous fish man."

Neither will we, I want to say, but I don't. What I say instead is "We should go that way, where the water gets deeper." And I point. "Somehow I just know that's where all the action will be."

We edge forward, our feet laboring through the deepening water. I reach into my pockets, hoping to feel the last of the warmth of the hot pebbles, but they are as cold now as the metal all around. I dump them in the water and keep wading on. In the light of our flashlights, I can see we're approaching a T-junction.

I'm about to make a comment about not losing our way when there's a gentle, flippery sound, somewhere behind us, and a soft throaty clicking.

I freeze and feel Violet do the same. Slowly we turn and bring our flashlights up.

There is something standing at the higher, drier end of the corridor. As our light hits it, we catch the gleam of scales, and I think at first it is Sebastian Eels in his chain mail. But then it blinks with two enormous spotlight eyes, and I know with dead certainty that it's not Eels. It drops into a low, menacing crouch, and double rows of webbed spines rise up along its back. Two long-fingered claws flex graspingly at us, and a mouth gapes open, edged with teeth like needles.

It's the malamander.

And it takes a step forward.

I'm just about to shout a very bad word indeed and explode into a million terrified pieces, when Violet does something amazing.

She speaks!

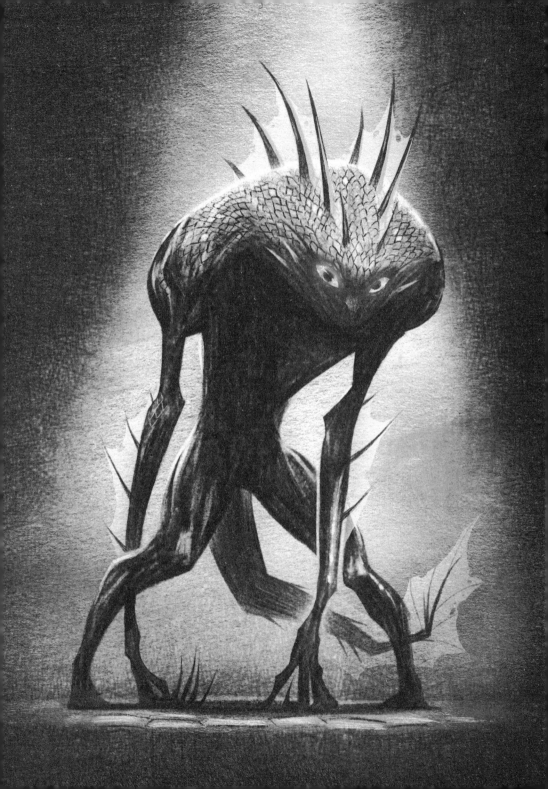

"It's OK," she calls out, trying to hide the shock and fear in her voice with a soothing tone. "We're not here to hurt you. We're friends, OK? Just friends. We mean you no harm."

She's holding out her trembling hands, showing one empty and the other holding the flashlight beam down.

The malamander stops and tips its head to one side, as if listening. It blinks again.

"It's OK," Violet continues, her voice growing calmer still as she gains confidence. "Everything's OK. We're here to help you."

And I think, *Bladderwracks! Vi is talking to it! To the malamander! This might actually work!*

The creature lowers its claws and makes a low, purring burble.

But then, just as I'm beginning to dare to breathe, there's a loud metallic *clang* from somewhere else in the ship.

The malamander jolts its head up. It opens its cavernous tooth-needle mouth and roars an earsplitting, soul-tearing, nightmarish cry of saurian fury.

Then it charges at us.

CHAPTER 36

THE BELLY OF THE BEAST

So we run. But just like a nightmare, our legs are heavy as we force them through the water, and we hardly move, and I know we can't escape.

And so this is it.

The end of Herbert Lemon, Lost-and-Founder at the Grand Nautilus Hotel. And of brave Violet Parma, too, who thought she could reason with sea monsters and change the world. There's nothing left to do now but decide if it's worth fighting for a moment or two of extra life, or if it's better to just fall down into the water and hope the end comes quickly.

I remember what Eels said about the sea being good for

disposing of bodies. I suppose that's true. Especially if the bodies are quite small—and devoured by a folkloric fish man in the belly of a sunken warship.

The malamander is not held back by the water as we are. If anything, it gains speed as it approaches, its fins slicing through the flood, its hands slapping at the sides of the corridor in its furious charge toward us.

My flashlight drops and I grip my Lost-and-Founder's cap with both hands and close my eyes as the monster leaps. I wait for the pain of the tooth-needle bite, for the rush of the venom, but . . . nothing. I open one eye and try to glance back without moving my head.

Still nothing!

Violet is crouching beside me, both eyes wide open.

"It jumped right over us!" she gasps. "It's gone!"

I stand up and stare down the corridor. The water in the T-junction is still swirling crazily where the creature passed. We can hear it screeching and clicking and scraping its way deeper into the ship.

I look at Violet.

"Eels!" we both say.

We wade forward to the T-junction and look to where the creature went. My flashlight must have blinked out when I dropped it, but Violet still has hers.

"How much time do we have?" she says.

I look at my watch. And gasp.

"We don't. It's quarter past ten. Low tide. We have about twenty minutes of slack water, tops, and then the tide will be coming back up. This corridor will be flooded again in half an hour."

"Then come on!"

The water is nearly waist-high here, and the cold is ferocious. As we wade forward we hear a new noise, a gusting human cry. I can't help hoping it's Eels getting his backside bitten by the beastie, but I recognize the cry-maker as Boat Hook Man. And the cry, which comes again, sounds triumphant. There's a fearsome answering roar from the malamander, and then all hell breaks loose somewhere in the dark ahead.

"They're fighting," I say as we push on.

The corridor ends in another T-junction, but there's no doubt which way we have to turn. The righthand passageway has corroded away altogether and widens out to an open space. The ceiling has gone, too, and several bulkheads, and we are standing at the entrance to a great cavern. The iron beams of *Leviathan*'s hull are exposed and curve overhead like giant ribs as we look into the belly of the sunken ship.

The cavern is one great pool of water, crisscrossed with half-submerged obstacles and twisted girders. At the far end, a glistening mound of seaweed can be seen, wreathed in mist.

"But . . . where are they?" Violet sweeps her flashlight here and there.

The water is swirling and writhing, and suddenly I know why the malamander and Boat Hook Man can't be seen.

"They're underwater," I say. "Still fighting. It must be really deep in here."

I climb onto a fallen beam, suddenly afraid to be up to my waist in this icy black pool.

"M-maybe we don't need to do this," I say to Violet, stammering with the cold. "The m-malamander will fight them and protect its egg. W-we should go back."

"Not yet," says Violet, and I see that she's shining her flashlight at that strange mound of seaweed at the end of the cavern.

"It's over there," she says, climbing onto a girder ahead of me and edging into the cavern.

"What?" I say. "The egg?"

"Yes, look!"

And so I look.

The seaweed mound is riddled with rotten things: moldy life jackets, slimy wood, and what look like bones. Human bones. But on the top of it, nestled in a slight dip, something glows with a dim red light that casts an eerie glow throughout the vast space.

"Well, well, well," says an echoing voice, and Violet halts still on the girder.

"Come to witness my moment of triumph, have you?"

A figure emerges from the water and begins to climb the seaweed mound.

It's Sebastian Eels.

"It isn't yours," Violet declares. "I won't let you take it."

"And I . . ." says Eels, raising his harpoon gun in a lazy motion and aiming it at Violet, "won't let you stop me."

"You won't shoot," says Violet.

"Really?" Eels leers at her. He seems to be enjoying the moment. "Now, why wouldn't I do that?"

"Because if you did, I'd fall in the water," says Violet. "And if that happened, you'd lose this."

And she pulls something out of her pocket and holds it up.

It's the ruby-red sea glass that Mrs. Fossil found, and which the doc used to lure the malamander to the museum — the stone that Violet took from Dr. Thalassi's dressing-gown pocket.

Violet is holding the flashlight in the same hand, in such a way that the light shines through the glass, making it glow a deep and magical red.

"But . . ." Eels's mouth drops open. His hands and the harpoon gun fall to his side as he splutters his astonishment. "B-b-but . . . how? How can you have the egg already?"

Then a look of dark fury passes over his eyes, and the harpoon gun snaps back up. But before he can fire, Violet flings the glass pebble far out over the flooded cavern.

It lands in the water —

Ploop!

— and vanishes from sight.

"The tide's already rising," she shouts. "You'll never find it in time."

"No!"

Eels scrabbles to get his mouthpiece in and the mask over his eyes. He turns on the head lamps as he runs back down the slimy mound and dives into the water.

And he's gone.

"OK, Vi," I say, giving a slightly desperate laugh of relief, "nice trick. Now we need to get out of here."

"Not yet, Herbie."

And Violet makes her way along the iron girder and jumps across to a buckled section of wall that is still above water. She runs across it deftly, then jumps onto the mound.

"Vi!" I shout, running to the end of the girder, waving my wristwatch in the air. "There's no time! We have to get out of here!"

"I can't go yet, Herbie," she calls back to me. And she climbs up the seaweed nest, toward the egg.

Cursing and gasping, I jump after her. I fall flat on the stinking mound, face-first, and then start to crawl up it through the bones and filth. By now I'm ready to drag Violet out of the ship if I have to. But when I get to the summit I see her crouching over the softly glowing egg, reaching her hands gingerly forward, as though she's afraid to actually touch it.

What are you doing? I want to say, but the words won't come.

The egg is astonishingly beautiful.

It's like a promise of all things wonderful.

It's like a crystallized dream.

Then Violet touches it and it blazes, casting an eerie dancing light over her wondering face.

"The malamander egg," says Violet to herself, not to me. "It's the malamander egg."

I shake my head clear. I look around. The water is definitely higher than it was before.

"Vi, we're leaving. Now!"

"No," says Violet Parma, lifting the fiery object with both hands and standing tall. "I have the egg at last."

CHAPTER 37

A WINDOW
TO THE PAST

"Violet," I say, hoping my voice sounds as if I won't take any nonsense, though I know it actually sounds desperate and squeaky. "What are you doing?"

"I'm sorry, Herbie," says Violet, "but this might be my one chance. This might be the only way I can find out what happened to my parents. My only way to find them."

"Violet, the tide is coming in," I say. "There is an angry man with a harpoon gun somewhere. There's another man with a boat hook for a hand, and somewhere, in case you've forgotten, is an enraged sea monster who cares very much about that thing in your hands. Now, I'm sorry about your parents, I really am, but if we don't get out of here *now*, we'll end up the same as them: gone — and never to be found again."

"No!" Violet cries. "Not *never to be found again*!"

And she stares into the crystalline surface of the egg.

"Show me," she murmurs, as if answering a question only she can hear. "Show me what happened."

The sea mist in the cavern begins to move, swirling toward Violet. More and more of it boils from the water as it gathers into a vortex that encircles the nest, moving faster and faster. The egg, still in Violet's hands, glows brighter than ever.

I want to tell Violet to stop. I want to knock the blasted egg out of her hands and bring her safely back to my little cellar in the hotel, with my leftover lunches and my cozy fire. But the sea mist is already like a tornado around us. All I can do is grab my cap with both hands and wonder what will happen next.

I don't have long to find out.

"Show me!" Violet is saying, louder now. "My parents. Show me!"

The mist twists, and a tunnel forms directly in front of us. An eerie silence falls as the tunnel widens. Then, through the tunnel, we can see an image — the beach at Eerie-on-Sea — bathed in moonlight.

I'm amazed to see such a thing, but part of my mind is still logical enough to wonder why we're being shown the beach at all. We could just go outside to look at that. But then I realize it's not *where* we're being shown that matters, it's *when*.

A man and a woman are walking up the beach. Behind them, I see the silhouette of the battleship *Leviathan*. It's Midwinter night, twelve years ago. It's the night Violet's parents disappeared.

The man is wearing a tweed jacket, which is soaking wet, a tie, spattered with sand, and rubber boots. He's also wearing a smile.

It's Peter Parma.

"Dad!" Violet gasps.

The woman beside him is wearing rubber boots, too, and a long raincoat. She also seems happy, despite being as wet through as her companion.

"Mum!"

But it's clear they can't hear Violet. Everything we can see through the tunnel is just a replay of past events.

"It's wonderful," says the woman. "A real live malamander! A completely new species never before described by science."

"Yes, Bron," says the man, putting his arm around her. "But you realize, of course, that you can never tell anyone. So you can forget naming it after yourself."

"I wouldn't dream of it!" The woman laughs. "Just knowing it's there—that such a thing is possible—that's enough for me. And as for the egg . . . !"

"The egg," says the man quickly, "has to be forgotten completely. No one should get ahold of something like that. The malamander lays it for someone else, for its mate. Who or what that mate is we may never discover, but no one must ever try to steal the egg again."

"But is it completely safe?" asks the woman. "With that creep Sebastian Eels after it?"

"Eels understands less than he thinks," says the man with a snort. "He knows it lays the egg on only one night of the year. And he knows it devours it the next morning. But he's an arrogant fool. I don't think he even realizes that the creature hibernates all summer."

The woman shakes her head.

"Technically, it doesn't," she says. "To hibernate means to sleep through the winter. The malamander sleeps through the summer, so the word you're looking for is *estivate.*"

"Don't get sciency with me, Bron." The man grins. "I'm immune."

"No, Peter, you aren't." The woman smiles back. "And you can't tell anyone either, don't forget. That means you can't publish your book. You've done all that work for nothing."

The man looks suddenly downcast.

"You're right," he says. "I can't."

"You give away too much. You even describe how to kill the malamander! Imagine if Eels ever got ahold of that information."

"Oh, don't worry about that." The man perks up. "I've hidden that particular page where he'll never find it. And as for the rest, well, I'll lock the manuscript away when we get home. Then, one day, I'll let Violet read it. When she's all grown up."

"We should get back," says the woman then. "I feel bad about leaving Violet with that friend of yours."

"We could hardly have taken a baby into the wreck of a battleship."

"No, but I don't really know your friend."

"Don't worry," says the man. "I've known Wendy for years. She's fine."

"OK, but . . ." The woman's voice suddenly takes on a tinge of anxiety. "Shouldn't we be able to see her by now? Didn't she say she'd wait over there on the harbor wall?"

The man takes a flashlight from his pocket and shines it someplace off to the side. Someplace Violet and I can't see, through this tunnel into the past.

"What woman?" Violet says, turning to me. "What woman are they talking about, Herbie? Who is Wendy?"

But all I can do is give a shrug to end all shrugs, and I look back at the scene before us. The scene where now Violet's parents are running.

"Wendy!" Peter Parma is calling. "Wendy, where are you?"

And then the scene switches to the harbor wall, where Violet's parents are staring down into the water below. Beside them are two pairs of shoes, but it's clear they have more urgent things to think about than changing out of their boots.

"Where is she, Peter? Where's our daughter?"

Peter Parma's face takes on a sudden expression of fear.

"Sebastian!" he says. "He said I'd pay a heavy price if I kept my discoveries from him. But surely he wouldn't . . ."

"What do you mean?" Violet's mum looks frantic. "He *threatened* you?"

"Wasn't there another boat?" asks Peter, pointing down the quayside to the water. A single boat is bobbing there. "There were two when we got here."

Just then, far out on the horizon, a motor coughs into life. A small fishing boat is just visible in a bank of approaching mist. It turns and heads out into the open ocean.

"Oh, dear gods!" Violet's dad gasps. "Sebastian, what have you done?"

Then Violet's parents are running.

"No!" says Violet, still clutching the egg and shaking her head. "This isn't right. I wasn't taken away in a boat; I was left in the hotel."

Now, through the tunnel, we see Violet's parents running down steps in the harbor wall to the small boat. In a moment, the engine roars and the boat—with Violet's parents aboard—speeds off to where the fishing boat has already vanished from view.

"Mum! Dad!" Violet calls, tears streaming down her face. "You've misunderstood. I'm right here! Don't go!"

But now both boats have disappeared in the bank of fog.

The scene fades as the tunnel collapses.

The mist begins to dissipate.

"No!" Violet cries. "This is wrong. I don't want to see the

past. I want to see *now*. I want to see where my parents are *NOW!*"

And her face twists in fury as she grips the egg even tighter.

The mist roars back around us, angry red now, whipping Violet's hair and nearly throwing me off my feet. A new tunnel starts to form.

I see something in the tunnel, something like trees—trees with giant leaves. There are two figures walking, stumbling, searching. The image begins to grow clearer . . .

But it doesn't get the chance.

The tunnel of mist breaks apart as Sebastian Eels bursts through it, his chain mail gleaming as seawater pours off it, his helmet lights blazing. He grabs the egg with one hand and punches Violet in the face with the other. Violet falls back, dazed, and slides down the slope of the malamander's nest.

She vanishes beneath the water.

And now Eels has the egg, his jubilant face bathed in its fiery red glow.

CHAPTER 38

CAPTAIN KRAKEN

Part of my brain—the part that is responsible for the squeak—goes into overdrive. But I ignore it.

Violet has just disappeared underwater.

And she hasn't come back up!

I heave a desperate gulp of stinking air into my lungs, race down the mound of wrack and rot, and throw myself into the water.

It's so abysmally cold and dark that I wonder for a moment if I've died without noticing. But then I bob back up and roll over. I reach down as far as I can, frantically swooshing my hand from side to side in the depths, and I find something. I don't have time to think about what it is. I just pull and pull and watch as

Violet bursts up through the surface, her face covered in seaweed and hair.

She gasps and coughs, and I try to swim with her, back to the corridor and to safety, but our clothes are too heavy with water, and the cold has its hand on my heart. I manage to shrug out of my coat and pull Violet out of hers, but we make no progress doing this, and it's all I can do to help Violet up onto the buckled bulkhead in the center of the pool.

I feel my foot wedge into a tight space deep underwater as I do this, and my trousers snag. I try to get up onto the bulkhead beside Violet, but it's no good.

I'm stuck.

All around, lit by the magical light of the malamander egg, seawater is spraying into the cavern as the tide continues to rise. We have just minutes to either get out of the wreck or learn to breathe underwater.

But my leg is stuck fast.

So this is probably the worst time for what happens next to happen. But it happens anyway. With a great burst of foaming water, the malamander surges up through the surface of the pool.

The monster is enormous, bigger even than I realized when it was charging us in the corridor. The spines on its back bristle and vibrate, and webbed ridges jut from its arms.

In its claws it is holding the broken body of Boat Hook Man.

The old sailor isn't dead—the curse must still be at work—but he has clearly lost the fight with the monster. His haggard face is white and awful above his yellow beard, and he lies helpless and foggy in the malamander's scaly arms.

Sebastian Eels, holding the egg, looks at the malamander. His face breaks into a sneer.

The monster, seeing the egg glowing in the man's hands, gives out a great shrieking roar and drops Boat Hook Man. It rises up in the water, throwing its arms wide as it prepares to lunge.

So Sebastian Eels shoots it.

Simple as that.

He drops to his knee, braces his gun, and releases one carefully aimed harpoon with a *th-TOUM* of compressed air.

The malamander quivers all over, its lunge suddenly ended before it began. The harpoon has buried itself deep between two of the monster's scales, where—now that we look closely—a slim opening in its armor can be seen.

Inside the opening, something is pulsing. It's the creature's heart.

The malamander gives another roar, weaker this time, so Sebastian Eels shoots again.

Th-TOUM!

Another harpoon, in exactly the same place.

Then *th-TOUM, th-TOUM, th-TOUM!* as three more find their mark.

Then there's a hiss of empty air as the auto-reloading gun runs out of harpoons. A look of alarm spreads over the face of Sebastian Eels.

But then he relaxes as he sees the malamander shudder violently.

Its arms fall, and it twists onto its back. The five steel shafts of the harpoons are clustered together in the gap in the monster's scales.

Straight through its heart.

With a gurgling sigh, the malamander twitches one last time and then goes still. As it slips beneath the water, its lamp-like eyes go dark.

It's dead.

"Not such a fearsome beast, after all," says Sebastian Eels, standing and replacing the harpoon gun in its holster. "Once you know where to hit it. What a shame you can't be here, Peter, to see this."

And he turns the fiery crystal egg in his hands.

There's movement in the water as something rises up beside the corpse of the monster.

It's Boat Hook Man.

He looks awful, his twisted body half submerged, his skin raked over with great gashes and slashes. He stares openmouthed at the body of the malamander. Then he turns to Eels.

"The egg . . ."

He reaches his arms like a beggar.

"Your promise . . ." he croaks. "Set . . . me free!"

"Ah, my old friend," says Eels. "I did indeed promise to free you from your curse. And you deserve it, I suppose, even though it was I who destroyed the monster."

"Set . . . me . . . FREE!"

Sebastian Eels holds the egg in his hands. He murmurs to it in a voice too low for us to catch, and its light blazes. Mist boils again from the water all around, swirling and twisting. But instead of gathering around Sebastian Eels on the nest, it encircles Boat Hook Man in the eye of a storm.

Before our astonished eyes we see Boat Hook Man lifted out of the water. His ruined form straightens, his wounds close up, his clothing mends. His beard shrinks back to a neat trim, and his face fills with color. The boat hook on the end of his right arm evaporates, and a new hand appears there, pink and perfect.

And now, where once had been a ghastly wreck of a human, a healthy and shipshape naval officer — in the prime of his Victorian life — is set down on a girder.

Boat Hook Man has gone, and in his place is Captain Kraken.

"It is a marvel," declares the captain, gazing over his remade body. "My nightmare is ended."

"Perhaps," says Sebastian Eels. "But, I wonder, has mine begun?"

"What do you mean by that?" says Captain Kraken.

"Well, you wanted the egg for yourself once," says Eels. "Perhaps you will try to take it again now."

"I paid the heaviest price for it," the captain replies. "I lost everything — my ship, my fine men, even my family, in the end."

"With the egg," Eels says, in a taunting voice, "you could wish it all back."

"Perhaps, but the egg is not made for the likes of you or I," says Captain Kraken. "I see that now. It will destroy anyone who tries to use it. I never want to see the damned thing again in my life."

"Ah," says Eels, with a leering smile, "then your wish is my command."

And he raises the egg, whispering to it.

Sea mist swirls again, and the water in the cavern starts to boil. But, no, it's not the water this time. It's something *in* the water.

It's the body of the malamander.

As we watch, the scaly corpse of the monster quivers and splits, and dozens of fleshy tendrils shoot up from it. They wrap themselves around the arms and legs of the astonished Captain Kraken and begin to pulse and thicken, becoming tentacles.

"What are you doing?" cries the captain. "You promised . . ."

But a purple tentacle slaps across his mouth and cuts off his words. The man struggles, but more and more tentacles are bursting from the sea now, wrapping him tightly, as the body of the malamander is transformed into a mass of writhing, quivering sea life.

"I think I liked you better with the hook," says Sebastian Eels, his face alive with fascination as he watches his terrible creations. "Or shall we try something else? A crab claw, perhaps?"

And with his words, mist swirls around the captain's new hand, which elongates and crusts into a blue-and-red crab pincer. At this the captain begins to struggle frantically. With a huge effort, he manages to cut through one of the tentacles holding him by using his new claw.

Eels, maybe sensing some danger to himself in this terrible game, whispers urgently to the egg in his hands. Light pours from the egg as the magic responds.

Captain Kraken's body trembles and ripples, then collapses into a mass of squid and jellyfish and sea slime. Now the water is filled with a riot of new sea life, splashing fins and writhing

tentacles. Something like an arm, with something like a giant crab claw at the end of it, reaches feebly toward Eels for a moment, but then it loses its form, tumbling into the water as sea urchins and starfish.

The light from the egg dims again, and the thrashing in the water dies down. The bodies of both the malamander and Captain Kraken are gone, transformed into countless sea creatures that swim away into the rising water.

"The power of life and death." Sebastian Eels gazes in triumph at the magical object in his hands. "My every wish made true."

"Is there a p-p-plan B?" I stammer to Violet, my teeth hammering together with the cold as I cling to the last of the bulkhead. "Now would be a g-g-good time for a plan B."

But Violet isn't there.

I look around groggily, this way and that. Violet has gone!

But then I see her.

She is swimming toward Sebastian Eels.

CHAPTER 39

A STRANGE AND EERIE LIGHT

Eels doesn't notice Violet coming, doesn't see her swim around behind the malamander's nest. He is still gazing in rapture at the egg in his hands, oblivious to the water that sprays in through the hull of the ship as the tide continues to rise. There's a slow boom as the first big wave hits the wreck. But then, why would the man worry about that? Sebastian Eels has the awesome power of the malamander egg. He also has full scuba gear. I can't see how anything can stop him now.

But there's still Violet.

I watch as she struggles up the mound of seaweed, where Eels still hasn't seen her. But she must have made a noise doing this, because his head jerks up and he starts to spin around.

So Violet shoves him.

It's a desperate shove, and it causes Violet to lose her footing, but Eels is caught unprepared, and he slips too. Violet grabs for the egg in his hand.

"No!" shouts Eels, raising the egg menacingly. But Violet somehow manages to break her slide down into the water and—with her mother's boots on—lands a kick in the man's face.

Sebastian Eels falls, dazed, back into the pool, the egg falling from his fingers.

Violet snatches it up.

She closes her eyes to concentrate, and I still have enough energy in my freezing brain to think, *What now?* Surely Vi isn't still trying to see her parents. Doesn't she know that we're as good as drowned already? None of that matters now.

The sea mist boils once more, red and strange in the submerging cavern, as Violet calls on the magic one more time.

"No!" Eels shouts again, splashing upright in the pool, grabbing his harpoon gun. He aims it at Violet, point-blank range.

Fut! Fut!

Since he didn't bother to reload the gun, the mechanism spits nothing but compressed air.

In desperation, Sebastian Eels starts climbing the mound, but by now Violet is wreathed in a maelstrom of power, and the

man slips back and cringes in terror as the light of the malamander egg grows brighter and brighter . . .

But then dims.

Violet lowers her hands, looking suddenly small and defeated.
The storm ceases its roar, dying down again, and the mist rolls
away.

Now all we can hear is the rush of water as the tide continues to rise. The magic is ended, and whatever it was Violet
wished for hasn't appeared.

"Nothing?" rages Sebastian Eels as he struggles back to his
feet. "You wretched, unimaginative child. Is that *it*? You don't
deserve the power. You are as weak and pathetic as your father.
Give me the egg! Give it to me now!"

"Are you sure you want it?" says Violet quietly. "Really sure?"

"Of course I'm sure." Eels rises up out of the sea toward her,
pulling his knife from its sheath. "Give it to me!"

"Then take it," Violet shouts, and she tosses the malamander
egg over the man's head.

Eels jumps, throwing himself up in a frantic bid to catch the
egg before it hits the water.

And he succeeds.

He bobs back down, holding the egg above him in triumph.

"Ha!" he cries.

And his cry is answered by a sound I thought I would never

hear again: a screeching, shrieking roar of reptilian fury. The malamander, miraculously whole again, glistening with iridescent scales and bristling with spines, leaps from the shadows and lands on Sebastian Eels. Its gaping mouth, lined as before with tooth needles, closes with a sickening crunch over the hand that holds the egg.

Then both monster and man are gone, crashing beneath the inky surface in a storm of water.

Which subsides.

There's a ripple or two, and a snaking finned tail twists to the surface of the water for a moment. Then there's nothing.

Sebastian Eels is gone.

Now all there is to worry about is the spraying of the invading sea, and the boom of the waves, and the creaking of the wreck as the tide rises to engulf us.

The water is up to my neck now. I make another attempt to free my ankle, but it's wedged fast and only hurts when I try.

I look over to the nest.

Violet isn't there.

"No, I'm here," she says, suddenly close.

I turn my head, and she's right beside me, treading water.

"You can still g-g-get out," I say, suddenly realizing it's true. "Just go, Vi."

"I can't leave without you," she says, and she dives down

beneath the water. But she's up again in a moment, gasping. There's no time left now, and no light in this ink-black sea. She needs to stop trying to free me if she's going to save herself.

"They'll be n-n-needing a new Lost-and-Founder at the G-G-Grand Nautilus Hotel," I say, pulling the remains of my cap from my head and pushing it through the water to Violet. "You should do it, Vi."

"Herbie, no!"

The water laps over my face for the first time. When it dips again I grab a quick breath.

"Please go, Vi," I say. "T-tell Lady Kraken . . ."

The water again.

Cof!

"Tell Lady Kraken . . ."

Then the water closes over me for good.

CHAPTER 40

WENDY

....

Bladderwracks, it's dark in here.

It's not cold, though, so I guess being as dead as driftwood has an upside.

Bit odd, though, isn't it? That I am able to think that? If I'm dead, I mean.

Perhaps I should try an eye. If I still have one.

So I do. And I have!

And what I see startles me wide awake.

A face is looking at me intently, from just a nose or two away. It's an impressive nose, too, a real Julius Caesar job. A pair of spectacles drops from the forehead of the face to land neatly on the hook of the nose, and a voice I know well says, "Ah, he's coming around."

"Dr. Thalassi?" I manage to say, but my chest and throat feel as if they're on fire, and I dissolve into coughs.

"Steady there," says the doc. "Don't try to speak, Herbie. Just take it easy."

"Violet?" I say anyway, springing up like a jack-in-the-box. "Where's Violet?"

I'm in a book-lined room, near a roaring fire. Something hairy and horrible is hunched over a typewriter in the window, and I realize where I am.

The Eerie Book Dispensary.

I'm lying on a makeshift bed of armchairs, wrapped in a blanket that smells of cat (but in a good way). Weak daylight is creeping in through the window, and I see that it's snowing.

"Morning?" I ask, in a voice like sandpaper.

"Morning," someone replies, and Violet appears at the doc's shoulder, her face beaming like the sun.

Then more people are there: Jenny Hanniver in her shawl, peering down at me. And Mrs. Fossil, her hands clasped together.

But there's something odd about them all. They look wet. Well, not actually wet, but as though they have recently been soaked to the skin and are now almost dry again. Jenny even has a piece of seaweed in her crinkly red hair.

I must look a bit confused, because Violet answers my question before I can ask it.

"They came to get us," she explains. "Mrs. Fossil sounded the alarm, after we left her on the beach last night, and all three of them came. Jenny swam like a fish, Herbie. It was amazing. She got your ankle free, and, well, here we are."

I swing my feet to the ground. I notice my Lost-and-Founder's cap is hooked on the log scuttle near the fire, but I leave it where it is for now.

"Eels?" I manage to say.

Dr. Thalassi makes a grunting sound in his throat.

"No sign of him. And after some of the things Violet has told us, that's probably just as well."

"We went to see him yesterday," says Jenny. "The doctor and I. We were worried he was planning something for last night, but we never thought he'd go this far."

"Herbie, *that's* who we heard talking with Eels," says Violet, "while we were hiding in his study." And the three adults gasp.

"It seems there's a lot more you haven't told us yet," says Jenny, folding her arms.

Violet gives a shrug and winks at me.

I say nothing. Sebastian Eels is a slippery character, but

surely even he couldn't have escaped that final malamander attack, not even in full scuba gear and armor. I shake my head. I don't want to think about that man ever again.

Violet coughs. The adults all seem to understand something from that cough, and they move away to the front of the shop to talk among themselves.

So now it's just Violet and me.

She passes me a cup of hot chocolate, and it feels like heaven as it slides down my half-drowned throat.

"I'm sorry," she says as I wipe my mouth. "I wasn't exactly honest about what I wanted."

"You mean about using the egg yourself?" I say, feeling as though Violet really doesn't have anything to apologize for. I should have expected it.

"I thought it could answer my questions once and for all," she says. "About what happened to my parents. But I should have told you first."

"If you had," I say, taking another sip, "would I have been able to talk you out of it?"

Violet grins.

"Probably not."

"Either way, you know what happened to your mum and dad now, Vi," I say. "For better or worse, the magic showed it to you."

"The magic showed me something," Violet agrees, looking

down, "but how do I know if that's what really happened? How would I know if the magic was just showing me what I *wanted* to see? Something to give me hope that I might see my parents again someday."

I shrug. There's really nothing I can say to that. Except . . .

"You brought it back, Vi." I lower my voice for this. "The malamander. When you had the egg that last time. Eels had killed it, but you wished it back to life! You remade the monster! When you could have had anything you wanted. Why?"

"Is it really a monster?" says Violet. "I mean, yes, OK, it's a monster, but that doesn't mean it's evil. As my dad said, the malamander lays its egg for someone else, not for us. No one should be allowed to just take it, Herbie. The magic is far too dangerous for people to use."

"But what if it bites someone again?" I say, thinking of Mrs. Fossil's hand. "The malamander is dangerous, too."

"It just needs space," says Violet. "It's a wild animal, after all, and like any wild animal, it just wants to be left alone."

"We can warn people to keep away from the wreck," says Dr. Thalassi, coming back over with the others. "It will just add to the legend."

"And, apparently, the creature hibernates for part of the year anyway," says Mrs. Fossil. "All summer long."

"Technically it's only hibernation if it sleeps in the winter," Violet corrects her. "The word you're looking for is *estivation*."

Dr. Thalassi blinks at her.

"How do you know that?"

"My mum told me," Violet replies.

"Well, well, well," says Mrs. Fossil, slightly breathlessly. "A new word for me, eh? All very interesting, very . . ."

"Is there something wrong, Wendy?" Jenny asks Mrs. Fossil. "You look flustered."

Mrs. Fossil gives a twitchy grin and swings her hands from side to side, as if she doesn't know what to do with them.

I look back at Vi, and then we both look at Mrs. Fossil.

"Wait," I say. "Mrs. Fossil, your first name is Wendy? I never knew that."

Wendy Fossil turns to Violet.

"And I only knew your *first* name," she says, her agitation beginning to overflow. "Herbie said you were named Violet, and I didn't make the connection, otherwise I would have said something, I promise. I didn't know you were Violet *Parma* until Herbie used your full name on the beach last night. And now I know that it's all my fault!"

And she sits down heavily in a chair, spilling a small cascade of beach pebbles and shells from her jacket pocket as she does so.

"My mum and dad left you to look after me?" asks Violet slowly. "The night they disappeared?"

"Oh, they did, they did!" cries Mrs. Fossil, clutching her knees. "They said it would be only for an hour or so. They said they wanted to walk down to the wreck of the battleship while the tide was out. It seemed romantic, so I didn't ask why. Your dad and I were old pals from way back, and I was out beach-combing for amber with my UV light, and I didn't mind having a little baby bundled in a sling inside my coat. It was cozy!"

"But what happened?" asks Vi, standing up. "What happened exactly?"

"That's just it," says Mrs. F. "I don't know. I agreed to be on the harbor wall when they got back. But, well, there was some good amber washed up that night, really grade-A stuff, and I suppose I walked a bit too far, or lost track of time or something. When I went back to meet them, they weren't there. Just their shoes!"

And she dissolves into tears.

"I never saw them again!"

Violet goes and stands over Mrs. Fossil. Then she puts her arm around her.

"It's not your fault," she says. "Maybe they lost track of time, too. Or misunderstood something. That's not hard to do when the tide is out and the mist rolls in."

Mrs. Fossil screws a well-used piece of tissue onto her nose and blows a honk.

"Afterward, when they didn't reappear, I went back to the hotel, but they weren't there, either. That's when I started to panic. I sneaked into your parents' room and left you in your crib. You were sound asleep. Then I made an anonymous call to the police."

"Anonymous?" I say. "But why?"

"I don't know what I was thinking," says Mrs. F. "I was just terrified it was my fault somehow. That wreck is so dangerous. And maybe it would look as though I were kidnapping you. I thought the coast guard would find them and that it would all be sorted out in a jiffy. Then, when it wasn't, when the police arrived, I was too scared to come forward. I'm so, so sorry."

"It's OK, Mrs. Fossil," says Violet, hugging her again. "Or may I call you Wendy?"

CHAPTER 41

ERWIN'S PAW

I don't know what it is that makes me look out the shop window just then. But look out I do, and I see in the thin light of dawn two figures—one sitting, one standing—near the statue in the middle of Dolphin Square.

I leave the others chatting and walk to the door, grabbing my Lost-and-Founder's cap as I go. I'm unable to quite believe my eyes.

Lady Kraken is there, in her bronze-and-wicker wheelchair. She's wearing a woolly turban and is tucked beneath a blanket embroidered with the crest of the Grand Nautilus Hotel. Behind her, standing to attention, is Mr. Mollusc. He's holding an open umbrella over Lady Kraken, to protect her from the falling snow.

I slip out of the shop and into the frigid air of the new day.

"Um," I say, as I stop before my employer, my heart galloping, "Your Ladyness?"

"I was watching," croaks the old lady, fixing me with her turtle eyes. "Last night, by the light of the moon, I was watching."

I nod.

"I saw you enter the creature's lair."

I blink.

"And now I have come for what is rightfully mine," says Lady Kraken, reaching out one clawlike hand, palm upward.

I know what she means, of course.

But did she really believe that I, a skinny twelve-ish-year-old, would be able to bring her the wondrous malamander egg?

And if she did, how will she react when she sees that I have nothing to give her at all?

Well, not exactly nothing.

I take my Lost-and-Founder's cap from my head and put it in her hand. Then I step back and bow my head.

I don't dare look at Mr. Mollusc. I can't bear to see his triumphant face.

Snow falls silently.

Eventually Lady Kraken speaks.

"It takes someone special, Mr. Lemon, to be Lost-and-Founder at the Grand Nautilus Hotel," she says. "I often wondered if I was right to give the position to you."

I say nothing.

"Many have wanted it," she continues. "Some have wanted it so badly that they have turned bitter when the chance passed them by. Isn't that right, Godfrey?"

Eh? I look up and find that Lady Kraken has turned to peer at Mr. Mollusc.

The hotel manager goes red and starts to splutter into his mustache.

"But, Your Ladyship, I assure you . . . that is to say, I have *never* . . ."

Lady Kraken silences him with her hand.

"It takes an honest heart to watch over the lost property of others." Lady K turns away from Mollusc and looks at me again. "And honest hearts are hard to find. I cannot afford to lose yours, Herbert Lemon."

She hands the cap back to me.

I put it on my head, and for once the elastic slips pinglessly around my chin.

"Just tell me one thing."

"Yes, Lady Madame?" I say.

"My grandfather, Captain Kraken, is he . . . ?"

And I nod.

"He is free," I say, thinking back to what happened to Boat Hook Man. "As free as the fishes. His curse is over."

Lady K sinks back into her chair with a long sigh.

"Then you have, after all, returned something to me that I haven't had for a very long time, Mr. Lemon. You have brought me peace."

She makes a regal circling motion with her hand.

"Come along, Godfrey."

Mr. Mollusc, avoiding my eye, grasps the wheelchair handles.

With a grunt of effort, he turns the contraption around and pushes it creakily across Dolphin Square and into the wakening town.

My legs are a bit wobbly as I head back inside.

"Are you OK?" asks Violet.

I manage a grin.

"I don't think I've ever been OK-er."

And so that's it. Just about.

There's a bit that comes next where cakes are brought out, and more hot chocolate is made, but I'm sure you can imagine all that for yourself. It's quite the little party.

A short while later, I manage to get Vi alone again. We're in the shop window, in front of the mermonkey. Its hat is held out to us, just a finger away. We both look up at its horrid grinning chops, and I can't help wondering if everything that happened to us would have happened differently if the mechanical beast had chosen a different book for Vi, back when she first came here. Or would it have all happened like this anyway, whatever the book? I suppose there's no way to know.

"So what happens now?" says Violet. "I think this is the end of the story."

"Could be," I say with a shrug. "Or it could be just the beginning."

Violet gives a shrug of her own.

"I suppose I'll have to go. Back to Great-Aunt Winniegar."

"Or," I blurt out, "you could not go! It kind of feels as though this is your place now, Violet. It kind of feels as though there's room in my cellar for two. I kind of wonder if maybe the Grand Nautilus Hotel could do with a *second* Lost-and-Founder—only we'd be more like detectives, in a kind of partnership, together, detecting cases and finding lost things and making everything all right again, one mystery at a time. Or . . . or something! I haven't worked it all out yet, but I'm, er, kind of wondering if you'd like that."

Then I stop, because all this came out in a rush, and I can tell I've gone a bit red.

"It's funny," says Violet with a smile. "I kind of had a similar thought, but I didn't know how to ask."

I grin.

"Of course, I can't promise another adventure like this one," I say. "Maybe this is the only interesting thing that will ever happen to us."

There's a purr, and we both look down to see that Erwin the cat has appeared and is entwining himself around our legs.

"Hello, puss," says Violet.

But Erwin says nothing.

Violet picks him up and holds him in her arms. He looks her in the eye. Then he reaches out a paw and taps the rim of the mermonkey's hat.

Its eyes light up.

And with a shrieking, smoking, mechanical riot, the mermonkey places the hat on its head, rises up on its iridescent fish tail, and begins to type.

ABOUT THE AUTHOR

THOMAS TAYLOR is an award-winning author–illustrator for children. He illustrated the cover for the original British edition of the first Harry Potter book and has since gone on to write and illustrate several picture books and graphic novels. He is the illustrator of the graphic novel *Scarlett Hart: Monster Hunter*, written by Marcus Sedgwick. Thomas Taylor lives on the south coast of England.

Return to Eerie-on-Sea
with the next book
in the series:

GARGANTIS

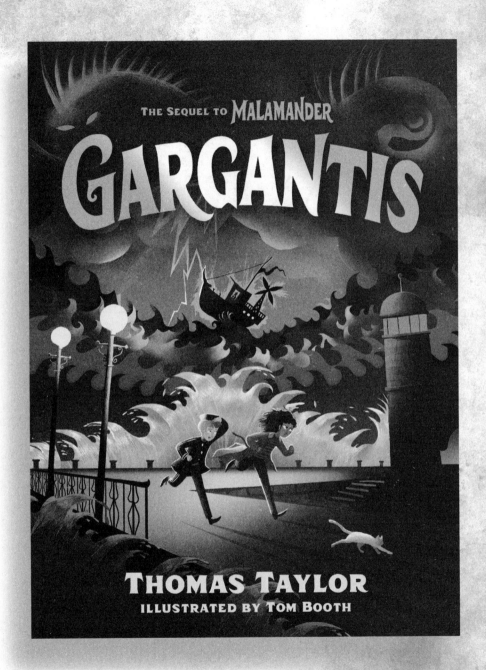

THE SEQUEL TO MALAMANDER

GARGANTIS

THOMAS TAYLOR
ILLUSTRATED BY TOM BOOTH

CHAPTER 1

DEEP HOOD

If there's one thing hotels have a lot of, it's strangers. Hotels are kind of in the stranger business, after all. But no hotel in the world puts the *strange* in *stranger* quite like the Grand Nautilus Hotel.

Take this guy, for example. The one who's just come in from the storm. The one walking across the empty marble floor of the lobby. See him? The one whose face is hidden by the enormous hood of a long waxed coat streaming with rainwater? He doesn't even pull his hood back to talk to the receptionist, and his luggage — a metal-bound wooden box clutched in one gloved hand — doesn't leave his side for a moment.

Who is he? What's his story?

What's in the box?

Of course, we'll probably never know. And that's fine. People are entitled to their privacy. Privacy is something else hotels have a lot of. Besides, there's something sinister about this man, something threatening that makes me *not want* to know, to be honest. I'll be quite happy once he's up in his room, doing whatever dark and secret things he's come here to do, far away from me. He takes his key and steps away from the reception desk . . .

. . . and starts walking in my direction!

I sit up and adjust my cap.

"May I help you, sir?" I say as the man in the overlong coat stops before the desk of my little cubbyhole. I look up and see nothing but darkness in that drooping hood. My cap starts to slip down the back of my head, so I straighten it.

"Herbert Lemon." A voice comes from inside the hood, and I flinch. There's an unnatural edge to that voice that makes my skin crawl.

"Th-that's right, sir," I reply. "I'm Herbie Lemon, Lost-and-Founder at the Grand Nautilus Hotel, at your service. Have you lost something?"

There's a sudden *KER-KER-BOOM* as a clap of thunder gallops around the town outside. The flash of lightning that rides with it only serves to highlight the darkness in the man's hood. The wind flings rain against the windowpanes, and the hotel lamps flicker.

The man remains motionless, dripping rainwater on my counter.

"Um-umbrella, perhaps?" I suggest.

I glance at the metal-bound box in the man's hand. There's barely room for a change of underpants in a thing like that.

"Or luggage, maybe?"

My voice is almost a squeak now.

The man leans in, his hood nearly closing over my head. My nostrils fill with the stink of wet coat and fishy breath.

"Do not ask what I have lost, Herbert Lemon," comes the man's voice, sounding as if each word is made with a great deal of effort. "Ask what I have found."

And that's when there's another crash of thunder and the hotel's lights go out.

Now, I know what you're thinking. Yes, you—sitting there safe at home, staring into your book with bugged-out eyes, waiting for something horrible to happen to me. You're thinking that I'm going to freak out now. And I admit, I am considering it. But you don't get to be Lost-and-Founder at the Grand Nautilus Hotel without learning how to be a professional. So, OK, yes, maybe I'm not the bravest mouse in the basket, but I am in *my* place, behind *my* polished desk, master of my own little world of lost property and shiny buttons. And so that's why, when the lights come back on again, I'm still sitting exactly where I was, clutching my Lost-and-Founder's cap with both hands and blinking at empty space.

Because, of course, the man with the deep hood has gone.

CHAPTER 2

WEIRDOS AND CRACKPOTS

The second rule of lost-and-foundering is *Keep calm and try a smile.*

Seriously, you'd be amazed at some of the things that turn up in my Lost-and-Foundery: thingummies, doodads, assorted hoojamfips of all descriptions. Once I even had a living, breathing human being hand herself in, but that's another story. You have to just take it all in stride, stay cool, and pretend that the Roman helmet, or false nostril, or bloodstained candlestick that got left in the conservatory is all in a day's work for a Lost-and-Founder. So it's the second rule I'm mostly thinking of when the hotel lights come back on to reveal that not only has Deep Hood gone, he's also left an object on my desk.

"You were just handing something in?" I ask the empty space where the man had been standing. "Why did you have to be so creepy about it?"

I lean out of my cubbyhole and see a trail of rainwater leading to the main staircase. If I wanted to, I could follow it and find out which room Deep Hood's staying in.

If I wanted to.

And the thing on my desk? Well, see for yourself.

It's a shell.

A strange, spiky shell—pearly white and spiraling around itself until it ends in a point. The small spikes, which are slightly curved, run up this spiral at regular intervals. I pick up the shell and peer into the trumpet end (it's one of those sorts of shells). It seems heavier than it should be, and it gives a clear metallic tinkle when I shake it. There's a small hole in one side, rimmed with brass. Is there something inside? Cautiously, I put the shell to my ear.

"I can hear the sea," I say to myself with a nervous chuckle of relief. "That means it's empty, right?"

"Or your head is," says an annoying voice, and I nearly drop the shell in surprise. From behind a large potted fern near my cubbyhole steps Mr. Mollusc, the hotel manager. He takes the shell from me.

"Shiny thing." His eyes light up. "Probably worth quite a bit.

What are you doing with something like this, Lemon?"

"It was handed in, sir," I say. "By that new guest."

At this, old Mollusc's horrible mustache bristles, and he almost throws the shell back to me.

"You spoke to him?" he says, nodding fearfully at the stairs. "He spoke to you?"

I shrug and hope that's answer enough.

Mollusc runs his fingers through his thinning hair.

"Why do we always get the strangest ones?" he asks, though mostly to himself.

I shrug again.

I mean, surely he knows the answer to *that* by now. Summer is a faded memory, and Eerie-on-Sea hasn't pretended to be a normal seaside town for so long that I wonder if it still can when the tourists return. Winter is lingering, and a storm mightier than any I have ever seen has engulfed the bay, turning the sea into a raging animal and blowing winds that would strip the enamel from your teeth. Only weirdos and crackpots would travel all the way to Eerie-on-Sea at this time of year. And where else are those weirdos and crackpots going to stay but the Grand Nautilus Hotel?

"Er, did *you* speak to him, sir?" I say, daring a question of my own. "His voice was a bit . . . you know. Did you think his voice was a bit . . . you know?"

"Don't be impertinent!" snaps Mr. Mollusc, suddenly remembering himself. "You have a new piece of lost property to take care of, boy. No doubt of great value. Kindly get on with your job."

And with that he turns on his heel and strides away.

Across the lobby, Amber Griss—the hotel receptionist—gives me a smile that seems to say, "Oh, don't mind him, Herbie. You know what he's like." But her raised eyebrow adds, "Just don't let him see you making that face!" So I grin an "Oops! You're right!" grin back and lift down the heavy old ledger instead.

This ledger is where I, and all the Lost-and-Founders before me, record everything that is handed in at the Lost-and-Foundery, as well as everything that is successfully returned. It's enormous. I heave it open and flip to the next blank space. I write the time and date and then the words PECULIAR SHELL. I'm not quite sure what else to write, to be honest.

Some of the hotel's clocks, the faster ones, start chiming for seven p.m. It's been a long day, so I just write, INVESTIGATION BEGUN AT 7-ISH next to PECULIAR SHELL. Then I close the ledger with a thud, flip the sign on my desk to CLOSED, and carry the strange shell down to my cellar.

The cellar is the real heart of the Lost-and-Foundery: a whole wing of the hotel's basement that generations of Lost-and-Founders have called home and that has long since become a glittering cavern of curiosities. Someone once described it as "Aladdin's cave," but it's not.

It's mine.

I shove a log into my little stove, hang my cap on a curly bronze whatsit, and flop down into my enormous armchair. The gale whistles through the chimney, and the walls quake with an almighty thunderclap, but the storm can't reach me down here. I grab my largest magnifying glass—itself a lost item—and use it to turn my eye enormous as I peer closely at the curious shell. And in particular at the small brass-lined hole.

"Something interesting?" comes a voice, and for the second time the shell nearly flies out of my hand in surprise.

"Can people please stop doing that?" I shout as the shadows move and Violet Parma steps into the firelight to sit beside me. She's holding a large white cat.

"Doing what?" she asks.

"Jumping out! I was just thinking how this place is mine-all-mine, and then you pop up from behind the lost pajamas and spoil it."

"You did say I could come around whenever I wanted," says Violet with a slight lift of her chin. "And there was a time when you invited me to live down here, remember?"

And both those things are true, even if the second one turned out a bit differently in the end.

But wait, you're probably wondering who Violet Parma is. Unless you've been to Eerie-on-Sea before, that is, and have heard all the stories about her. And if *that's* the case, then let me tell you that those stories are also true. I know because I was there for most of them. But whatever you've heard, and whatever I say, and whatever you think of this wild-haired, brown-eyed girl with a cat, all that really matters right now is that Violet is my best friend here in Eerie, and she knows how to open my cellar window.

"Besides," says Violet, "the storm is worse than ever. Poor Erwin here got lifted right off his paws and was nearly swept out to sea! I didn't think you'd mind us hiding out down here for a while." And she puts Erwin—that's the cat, by the way—in his favorite box of lost scarves, the one I keep near the wood burner.

"You've got something new," Violet adds, staring eagerly at the iridescent shell in my hands.

"There's a hole in the side." I flip the shell around. "I was just going to look in it, to see—"

"Great idea!" Violet takes the shell and the magnifying glass from me, and now she's the one with the giant eye, peering into the hole in the shell.

"There *is* something in there, too."

"What sort of something?" I ask, deciding not to protest.

"In the bottom of the hole." Violet's eye looks bigger than ever as she leans into the magnifying lens. "There's a piece of metal, like a little pin with squared-off sides. Like the kind of thing you see when you look into the winder hole of an old-fashioned clock."

"Like the kind of thing that's turned with a key?"

"Exactly," says Violet. "You have some of those keys, don't you? Herbie, I think there's clockwork in this shell!"

I open the large toolbox beside my repair desk, heave out a big jar, and carefully tip its contents into the pool of light from my lamp. From the jar spills keys of every kind. It takes a bit of poking about, but eventually I find a brass winder key that neatly fits the hole in the shell.

"Well?" says Violet when I don't turn the key. "What are you waiting for?"

"Maybe we shouldn't," I reply. My mind goes back to the creepy man who left this shell, with his disturbing voice and drooping hood. "I'm supposed to keep things safe, Vi, not mess around with them. Maybe it wouldn't be right to wind this thing up."

"Are you serious?" Violet blinks at me. "How can you not be curious to see what it does?"

"I am curious, but . . ."

I glance over toward Erwin and see that the cat, while in every other way appearing to be fast asleep, has one ice-blue eye wide open and is staring at us intently. It looks as though Erwin is on Violet's side, as usual.

"I just wonder if . . ."

"Oh, give it to me." Violet takes the shell again.

She turns the key.